OF
VENGEANCE

OF
VENGEANCE

J.D.
KURTNESS

Translated by Pablo Strauss

DUNDURN
TORONTO

The translator, Pablo Strauss, thanks Aleshia Jenson for an illuminating first edit, and Kate Unrau for her copy edit.

Acquiring editor: Scott Fraser | Editor: Kate Unrau | Cover illustration and design: Sophie Paas-Lang
Printer: Marquis

Library and Archives Canada Cataloguing in Publication

Title: Of vengeance / J.D. Kurtness ; translated by Pablo Strauss.
Other titles: De vengeance. English
Names: Kurtness, J. D., 1981- author. | Strauss, Pablo, translator.
Description: Translation of: De vengeance.
Identifiers: Canadiana (print) 20190053348 | Canadiana (ebook) 20190053364 | ISBN 9781459743755
  (softcover) | ISBN 9781459743762 (PDF) | ISBN 9781459743779 (EPUB)
Classification: LCC PS8621.U785 D413 2019 | DDC C843/.6—dc23

1 2 3 4 5   23 22 21 20 19

We acknowledge the support of the Canada Council for the Arts and the Ontario Arts Council for our publishing program. We also acknowledge the financial support of the Government of Ontario, through the Ontario Book Publishing Tax Credit and Ontario Creates, and the Government of Canada. We acknowledge the financial support of the Government of Canada through the National Translation Program for Book Publishing, an initiative of the *Roadmap for Canada's Official Languages 2013–2019: Education, Immigration, Communities,* for our translation activities.

VISIT US AT

 dundurn.com | 🐦 @dundurnpress | 📘 dundurnpress | 📷 dundurnpress

Dundurn
3 Church Street, Suite 500
Toronto, Ontario, Canada
M5E 1M2

Revenge is sweet.

1

Standard Introduction

Let's be honest: Who hasn't fantasized about shooting someone in the face with a hunting rifle? It doesn't matter why. In the heat of the moment, one reason's as good as the next. When the reasons still seem good after enough time has passed, I take action.

Every day I look a murderer in the eye. There she is, through the looking glass. An inverted image of the same person standing on my side of the mirror. I'm a murderer; the murderer's face is my face. *Voilà*. I know exactly what a murderer looks like. Hey, friend.

I look myself in the eye, hands resting on the rim of the sink, and perform my daily affirmation. "I'm a murderer." It's my own personal version of "I'm good enough. I'm smart enough. I can do this." My lips move and, depending on the words I say, a few teeth appear. The same ones that show when I smile.

I recite each word slowly, either in my head or ever-so-quietly out loud. Sometimes I take a chance and say it slightly louder, in my normal speaking voice. I like the sound of my own voice. It's a murmur in my silent apartment, slipping out of the bathroom only to be drowned out by the electrical hum in the walls. I listen to the irregular clicking of the baseboard heaters, generating heat without the slightest concern about who I am.

Another reason for this daily ritual: I'm scared of forgetting who I am. Sometimes life is good, and I take breaks.

It's a summer afternoon. I'm twelve, finished with elementary school. I've been on summer holidays for three weeks now, and I'm hanging out down by the river. There's nothing I enjoy more than spending entire days outside, coming home only to eat. Sometimes I even skip meals, though my parents disapprove. I come home when evening falls and it gets hard to see. Get some sleep and head right back out the next day. Eighteen hours of daylight is my version of bliss.

I'm in a place I think of as my spot. There's a tree that's perfect for climbing, with three branches in all the right places: one under my ass, one to prop up my feet, and a third to rest my back on. Together they form a chair of sorts. I have a nice view of the little river flowing through a ditch down below. I can also see the opposite bank. If I stretch, I enjoy an almost unobstructed 270-degree view all the way to the cemetery, where the trail runs. I can't see behind my position, but that's no big deal; all that's out that way is forest too dense to play in this time of year. Beyond the forest is a city park, but no one really bothers with it — why would you, with all this pristine nature, teeming with life?

Up in my tree, no one can see me. Sometimes I pack a lunch. I make my own. My parents think I'm responsible and have stopped worrying that I'll starve to death. I'm almost a teenager, so it only makes sense that I've more or less stopped talking to them. That's their theory, anyway.

I wrap my food in nonreflective packaging. No aluminum foil, no plastic bags. I watched a movie once where the murderers caught sight of a witness because of a ray of light that reflected in the lens of her binoculars. That won't happen to me. I also steer clear of sunglasses. They're just one more thing to carry around, one more thing I'd probably lose anyway. Noise isn't such a big deal up here. It's okay to open a container, move around, let out a sigh. The river drowns out most sounds. Except for screams.

I found my spot last week. I was out early to do a little scouting before anyone else showed up. Sometimes I arrive too late, and there are already people at the river bank or the path leading up to it. When that happens, I turn right back.

One morning, eight days ago to be precise, I got here early enough one day to find a nice quiet spot. Just the kind of place no one would think to look. Eureka: the perfect tree. Next to it was a large rock that I could stand on to reach the higher branches. It was a massive balsam fir that had by some miracle survived an entire century without being massacred at the altar of Christmas. An old, almost dead tree with barely any remaining trace of scent and not a lot of sap to stick to my clothing. Sap smells great, but it's hard to get off your clothes, so I stay away. I don't want hassles with my mom.

I've been counting the days since I found my tree: eight. I count a lot of things. The number of kids down below, the tiles on my ceiling, the holes in my runners, the exact number of seconds it takes an egg to cook so the yolk is still a little runny but not slimy. Careful planning minimizes the chances of nasty surprises.

My first time was a stroke of random luck. I responded with sound reflexes, and discovered the sheer pleasure of it. Now I come mentally and physically prepared, and bring all the equipment I could ever need.

I'm still startled every time I catch a glimpse of myself in a window, a mirror, or a photograph. My face is all wrong. Some might put it differently; they'd say I have the perfect face. My theory is that I was born with someone else's face, and my real one is off somewhere else, attached to the wrong soul.

I just don't look the part. My face should be angular, striking, and slender, with that sickly pallor certain men find irresistible. But the allure of the mysterious *femme fatale*, that image we're bombarded with day in and day out, just isn't me. I'm fresh-faced, with the most innocuous features imaginable. I emanate innocence and wholesome pleasures, like farmers' daughters advertising milk or girls on the packaging of anti-acne medication. Just like them, my pores breathe healthily. I have slightly rounded features, a ready smile, straight teeth, and smiling eyes. Even the beginnings of crow's feet, if you look closely. My pale skin turns rosy in the wind, or in the cold, or when I exert myself. My cheeks are like scrumptious fall apples. People have been saying it since I was a little girl. All the hours I spend outside, plus these freckles: How could anyone imagine I'm not an exemplary young woman?

Where did that other face end up, the one that should be mine by rights? What happened to that pointed jaw, those big feverish eyes and salient cheekbones? Who got that intimidating head of hair? Was my soul mixed up with another in some limbo, like babies switched at birth in a Latin-American hospital?

I wonder if ugly people feel the same way: startled by their own reflections in the mirror, disgusted by an unattractiveness no amount of torment will ever inure them to. Do they feel the same confusion I do after performing certain acts? Are they, like me, unable to believe that the symmetry of their faces remains unchanged? If my outward appearance reflected my inner self, I'd look dangerous, like the bad guys who get killed off at the beginning of the movie: dark-skinned cannon fodder, balding villains, disfigured hoodlums, random henchmen. I might also give off that whiff of danger, but I have to face facts; I just don't. My pheromones collide with those of other people without causing so much as a ripple. Yet the real danger is her. This woman I spy from the corner of my eye in every window I pass. She's there in the bathroom, just above the sink. She's the one staring at me innocently.

I look like a nurse, or a librarian, or a soccer player. My face is my best alibi.

I guess I should start at the beginning. But I don't even know who I'm speaking to. Let's assume you're a creature of the future since the present is already past. I'm going to call you a creature; why not, since woman and man are two categories on their way to joining the theory of humours in the dustbin of history. Perhaps you're nothing more than a puddle of lipids. Or a brain in a jar. Maybe my text has been converted into electrical impulses, predigested by an intelligence unconnected to any other organ, floating in a nutrient-rich, conductive liquid medium. Are you a child? A citizen of the People's Republic of China, our world's reigning superpower? An intergalactic refugee?

Or maybe nothing has changed — yet. In that case you may be a reader in the near future. You could be my neighbour, my employer, my friend. I'd still prefer to imagine a reader from another era. I don't want to hurt anyone I know. No one chooses to dump bodies where they might poison their wells.

I choose to live dangerously, and one day I'll push it just a little too far. Statistically speaking, my life will be a short one. But then, it's all relative: if we lived in the time of the Black Death, I'd already be in the twilight of my life. Or dead from childbirth, or from the pneumonia I had when I was five. Without modern medicine we'd all be dead, with our flabby bodies, giant heads, and feeble eyesight. Not to mention our rampant anxiety.

At any rate we've got no more than ten or fifteen years until every one of us is monitored, from egg to cremation urn — and even before, even after. Unless you take precautions, that future is here. I take precautions. My goal is to have fun while meting out a little justice here and there before we get to the ending where we all get swallowed up by the all-seeing omnipotent System.

So let's begin our story on that particular afternoon — an afternoon that also marks, I now realize, the end of my childhood. The sun is still high in the sky, but it's not too hot. Maybe twenty-four degrees. There's a cool, gentle breeze blowing in from the north. I can feel the sun through my clothes and on the back of my neck, where it's filtering through the leaves of the trees all around me. It's all so pretty. And everything smells so good: the wind, the old fir tree, me.

Even back then, perched in my tree, I was thinking about you, people of the future. I try to put myself in your shoes, imagine I know everything. Like other kids my age, I watch TV, and I believe I'm witnessing something big, the end of something precious: the earth as we know it, fresh air, clean running water, the birdsong slipping through my window. All this is going to disappear because we're not recycling enough and we're pillaging the Amazon rainforest. And because some crazy bastard set a giant mountain of tires on fire in Saint-Amable, Quebec.

Describing our own era is never easy. We focus on what seemed important at the time. We leave out the fabric of everyday life, which reveals much more than our philosophy. The example I give, in my imaginary conversations with entities from other places (other times, spaces, space-times), is that virtually everything we eat has at one point been wrapped in plastic. The seeds in their packaging. The plant roots in the tarp that keeps them moist and warm. The produce in its little transparent plastic bag, which is then placed in another larger plastic bag along with the rest of the food, and then under a layer of Cellophane if there are leftovers, or to be reheated, before finally ending its life in the little kitchen garbage bag, whence it is transferred to the larger plastic garbage bag. Meat's no different. It comes on a Styrofoam tray wrapped in multiple layers of Cellophane; sometimes the cut is squared away between two thick layers of plastic melted together and sealed sous-vide.

Let's not forget our bottles of juice, and water, and soft drinks. Some people have even had the nerve to put milk in plastic bottles, rendering it undrinkable. Families usually get their milk in three-packs of clear plastic bags, which are, of course, enclosed in a fourth coloured plastic bag printed with all the vital information the smaller plastic bags omit.

There's more: our cookies and crackers, ice cream, pasta, and myriad other products that have all been processed in one way or another before making their way into our pantries, after being shrewdly arranged on the shelves in the aisles we walk down with our metal shopping carts because carrying our own food over any substantial distance has become an impossibility. We no longer have the willpower or the muscle power.

Back then I was certain that, no matter what the reassuring pamphlets said, our Gentilly power station would be the next Chernobyl. The CANDU company that made our friendly neighbourhood reactor came to our school to tell us all about the marvels of nuclear power. Their technical knowledge was so advanced they were certain no accident was possible. The radioactive waste was being dumped under our impenetrable Canadian Shield, well-protected from even the worst catastrophes. I didn't believe a word of it. I was equally convinced that acid rain would eat away at everything and destroy our lakes. Today we've almost stopped talking about it. News is, by definition, a break in the continuity. When people are constantly dying, and have been for generations, the media gets bored. And so do we.

But look on the bright side: I live in an age of wonders, with a plethora of technological marvels and the leisure time to accomplish great things, should I so choose. We're still free, still entitled to privacy. People with something to hide can still do so. I can deceive and lie with impunity. I frequently put these few powers of mine to the test. The one I'm most proud of is my invisibility.

I make my living exercising a profession that will one day be as obsolete as log driver and telegraph operator. I'm a translator. The day will come when computers will learn to understand irony, context, everyday life, humour, and the other wonders of human nature. Then we translators will go the way of the dodo. For now, though, even bad translators like me can still earn enough to eat and pay rent. Like everyone else, our days are numbered.

2

Fiset

Let me get to the point of my story about the fir tree and the river. His name is Fiset.

There was a drowning in Dupuis Creek that summer. I should mention that I only learned that the trickle of muddy water snaking through the ditch was called Dupuis Creek by reading the newspaper story. We always just called it "the River." Just like the other river, which we call "the Other River." Passing on the finer points of local toponymy isn't a priority of parents around here.

So as it happens, "the youngster Fiset" was in my grade-six class. Another error missed by the newspaper's fact checkers: see, the boy in question was actually known as "Fat Fiset." At least, that's what everyone in my grade called him. As for the older kids, I doubt they had a name for him at all since they had a Fat Fiset of their own. Our Fiset was his little brother.

In elegiac prose the daily paper informed us that one Dave Fiset, five foot eight, drowned in a three-foot-deep creek. Which is accurate. Dupuis Creek is thirty-eight inches deep at its shallowest point, and it doesn't really have a current. "An unfortunate incident that should give the entire community pause and make us reflect on the importance of never letting young children play alone near a body of water."

I remain convinced to this day that no one will ever drown in Dupuis Creek again. Not without a little assistance.

I go down to the river for a little peace and quiet. It's been raining all morning and it just stopped, so there's still no one there when I get to the riverbank. Thanks to the wind, the mosquitoes aren't even that bad, for such a humid day.

I have a book to read in case there's no one to observe, and my plan is to spend the afternoon in my tree. From the moment I get there and start tying my backpack to a branch, I hear them coming down the trail. I look over to the cemetery, and who should I see but the Fiset brothers. I have plenty of reasons not to like these guys.

To name three, they're ugly, they smell, and they're constantly yelling, a habit they must have picked up from their equally obnoxious mother. You can hear her all the way across the supermarket parking lot.

Everyone in my class prays they won't have to sit next to Dave Fiset. At the end of the school year, when the days grow warm, it gets excruciating. A bizarre odour that clings to the roof of your mouth. At first you don't notice it, but little by little the air grows heavy and saturated. The teacher pretends not to notice, but you can tell she's holding her breath whenever she walks by him. It smells like my uncle's Ski-Doo helmet, which he lent me once so I could go for a ride with my cousins. Like that, but worse.

Fat Fiset also enjoys digging deep in his nose and then laying out his hard-won treasure for all to see. If anyone else dared do that, it would be a one-time thing: they'd get harassed so badly they'd have to change schools, move to a new town, maybe leave the country altogether. But the usual rules don't apply to Dave Fiset. Dave has the skills to defend himself, zero parental supervision, and a few screws loose. Everyone can feel it. There's only one way to handle Dave: like a wasp. You ignore him until he eventually goes away.

Dave repeated grade three. That's why he's older than everyone else. He's the kind of kid who, come grade six, can barely read but knows exactly what to do to put the fear of death into anyone who would even think about ratting him out. A real monster. Today we have a word for the modus operandi of the Dave Fisets of the world: bullying, a.k.a. the art of making poor kids' lives miserable. But back then it was just a normal part of life, like worrying about the hole in the ozone layer. And just like that once-pressing environmental issue, all the summits, conferences, and marches in the world won't be enough to make bullying a thing of the past.

I watch them. Dave's big brother has gone on to high school now, though word is they only passed him because no one could bear the thought of Fiset senior running wild in elementary school another year. He must be in a special class now with the rest of the county's lost causes, chomping at the bit until they park him in a professional program for future sanitation workers.

And that's the sum total of what I know about the Fiset brothers. They don't leave the house much. They must have killer video games. Usually I know a little more about people, but those two gross me out too much to inquire further. At this point I still haven't grasped the importance of gathering information on my enemies.

Out in the forest, Dave's having a gay old time, uprooting plants on the banks and stomping on tadpoles, while his older brother is busy catching garter snakes to burn with his magnifying glass. The guy basically burns whatever he can get his hands on: grass, tadpoles, the poor garter snake he finally catches, his brother's arm. This last one causes a bit of a kerfuffle, but the two brothers make up by having Dave burn his older brother's arm to even things out. Without a doubt, those two are bound for glory.

My afternoon is ruined. Coming down from my perch is out of the question: the risk of being seen or heard is too great. The last thing I want is for the numbskull and his idiot brother to realize I'm out here all alone in the woods with them. I'll just have to put up with them until they get tired and head off to go kill something else.

I read a few pages, but it's like doing homework while your dad's watching boxing on TV: the prospect of a massacre keeps distracting you; there's just no way to concentrate.

Then, through some sort of miracle, the shouts die down. I look down and Fat Fiset is all on his own. His big brother is walking up the path to the cemetery. He must have some tombstones to spit on. Dave has his pants down, taking a serious dump on the river bank. His back is turned to me, so I can finally climb down. Thank you, constipation. They must not be getting enough fibre since he's been squatting for a good five minutes. I can see a few dark hairs growing out of his crack. I have time to think.

The plan I come up with is this: find a rock, throw it, crouch down behind a bush, and have a good laugh while I watch the dude try to figure out what hit him. I'll aim for his big hairy white ass. I'm already laughing. My position is higher in elevation than the banks. I have a clear shot, and he won't see me. His ass is ridiculously exposed: the perfect target. He'll think it's his big brother messing with him.

I throw with all my might, like a baseball player. I don't stick around, not even long enough to see where it lands; I'm already rolled up in a little ball, hiding. I count to ten before I move.

Then I look for an opening in the foliage to watch the story unfold, but I don't see Fiset. Shit. Where is he? I can't hear anything unusual: no one scrambling around, no one swearing. I count to one hundred. Still nothing moves. I pull my hood down over my baseball cap for better camouflage. My hoodie is green, but my cap is beige. I crawl over. Keep my eyes on the ground, to avoid making anything crack. When I finally summon the courage to stand up, Dave Fiset is floating ass-up between two big rocks in the creek.

Thinking back, I remember his hair undulating around his head, like a jellyfish or seaweed. And I remember thinking that jellyfish lived in salt water, not rivers. Funny what runs through your mind at times like those. I was disappointed. Things hadn't gone according to plan. There was no way I could tell anyone what had happened. What I'd done would look callous in hindsight. I'd be hard-pressed to find anyone to laugh at my hilarious joke.

I left. Put on my backpack and set off on a big detour, in the hope of avoiding the other Fiset brother. I took off behind the Dubé farm to pick some strawberries, up on the headland where there's too much wind for trees to grow. The headland is an empty tract of land that must belong to someone, but no one knows who. A no man's land where older kids go to make campfires, and finders keepers is the only law. The morning rain had done its work; you could almost hear the berries ripening along the ground. The ants were industriously fighting over the same spoils. My parents liked to joke that they made a great strawberry-ant pie.

As I thought about what I had done, a sense of satisfaction stole over me, almost a feeling of euphoria. The beaming sun helped. My initial disappointment metamorphosed into something more joyful. No one would ever know it was me. My fingerprints were nowhere to be found. And no one had any idea where I hung out on nice days like that one.

I didn't see what happened, but I did have a theory. Obviously my aim was off. Instead of hitting Fiset's ass, I must have hit him on the back of the head, and he must have gone down like a clotheslined hockey player. He was already squatting, so the impact knocked him over. Then his head hit one of the big rocks along the bank. Without a sound. Or rather the sound of his fall was lost in the burbling of the creek and the rustling of leaves in the wind.

The only downside, aside from the impossibility of boasting about my great work, was that Fat Fiset would never know who took him out. Sitting there in the headlands, I wondered whether he was really dead, though I didn't have the courage to go see for myself. I was afraid his brother would come back before I managed to get away. I'd have to wait for the news. I'd have to act surprised.

Even before casting the stone, I had a fleeting vision of myself kneeling on Fat Fiset, cleaving his skull with a big rock. Sitting in the beating sun, another vision of that moment came back to me. I pictured myself as the caveman in *2001: A Space Odyssey*, but instead of using a bone, I'd bash his head in with a rock from the river bank. It's all there in my mind: the arc of the water following the movement of my arm, my other hand sliding along my victim's throat, holding him still as he tries to bite my fingers; the muffled thud of the rock hitting his temple; the kickback in my arm, like when you drive a nail; the swell of triumphant music, the rhythm of mallets battering kettledrum.

Sure, I know what actually happened: I threw a rock from the top of the bank. It flew through the bush I was hiding behind. It landed in just the right spot. End of story. When would I get the satisfaction of looking into the eyes of the person I hated in the moment before I ended his life? Maybe never. I'd have to be content to lie here in the middle of a field of fragrant berries with my nose buried in my forearms, fantasizing about the perfect crime before the horseflies got too bad.

And my forearms smelled good. A comforting blend of tanned skin, earth, and musk. I never pick all the berries I can find. My dad taught me to leave some for the birds. It's tempting not to heed his advice when you're as methodical as I am. But I like birds.

Deep in my wild strawberry patch, I watched the ants at work. I forced myself to calm down. I couldn't go home all shaky and hopped-up on adrenalin in the middle of a nice summer afternoon. People would suspect something.

I waited for the sun to go down behind the silo in the distance, signalling that afternoon was over and it was time for dinner. I went home. It was almost 7:00 p.m.

I brought a baseball cap full of strawberries. My mom was mad because they had stained the outside of the cap, so I told her I'd soak it myself with a little bleach. And that was that: my first murder. I got in trouble for the stain on my cap, but it was nothing a good soak couldn't take care of.

The detectives questioned everyone: neighbours, friends, parents. Were the brothers fighting? Had a sexual predator tried his luck and then run away after his victim got too shaken up? Had anyone seen anything? No, maybe, no.

After that we weren't allowed to play by the river anymore. In fact, we kids were barely allowed to go outside to play without our parents. The predator was still at large, if you could believe the rumours flying around. No one seemed to grasp the absurdity of the idea that someone might want a piece of Fiset's ass. Or maybe that was what made the whole affair so sordid: only the most perverted of deviants would go after that particular ass.

My parents, simple, sweet, hard-working people that they are, were horrified that such an act could have occurred in what was basically their own backyard, where their own daughter was in the habit of hanging out. Let's just say the fresh-picked strawberry pie didn't go down easily.

We moved in August, around two weeks before the new school year. I'd never have to see anyone I knew from my old school again since our new house was in a different district. It was a fresh start for us, far from the troubled waters and the depraved maniacs lurking in the woods. I was relieved we were leaving because every time I ran into Mrs. Fiset at the supermarket, she gave me a hug. Since Dave and I were in the same class and lived in the same neighbourhood, she'd picked up the notion we'd been friends. She was even more haggard than before, if such a thing were possible. She had always looked as though she'd been up all night, with her hair sticking out all over the place and eyes crusty with makeup. Now she wasn't even bothering to put on foundation; her skin was straight-up grey instead of her usual greyish-orange hue.

Some people claim to be visited by an angel. Others hear God speak to them. Still others watch documentaries on chimpanzees. In every case, it takes a stroke of luck to find your vocation. I might have spent my whole life searching. Hare Krishna? Hairdressing? Water polo? But the universe blessed me with a taste of the perfect crime. The next steps would be more difficult, but over time I learned that there is such a thing as impunity. I just had to keep my light hidden under a bushel.

3

Spray-Foam Insulation

Everyone loses their mind in a heat wave. Especially in the city. Melt, polar ice caps! Lay waste to our lowland cities! Blow, hurricanes! Get it over with! We deserve it.

It's one of those days when I break into a sweat just sitting on a chair in my kitchen. I'm fasting because I'm not willing to open the fridge. If I do, the ambient heat will thwart all its efforts to stay cold. The fridge is groaning and blowing hot air out the back to join the mass of hot air already filling the room. It's been running at full tilt for three days now. On the rare occasion it does stop, it trundles to halt like a quivering beast and rattles my dishes. Then, after a moment of silence, it fires right up again.

It's my first summer in the apartment. I swear it'll also be my last. I'm happy that I chose to live alone, now that

I understand why the rent was so cheap. The place is a sauna. Everything's heavy and sticky. I'm on the fifth floor of a glorified henhouse. I can't scrub away the tobacco smell the previous tenants kindly left behind. We should just go ahead and shoot all smokers. They make everything stink and cost our health-care system a fortune.

The stench outside is every bit as ripe: a mix of old garbage and alley piss. There's a bush in the corner that the local dogs can't get enough of. When it gets to the point where even I can pick up on the little messages they send each other, it's time for rain. So why don't I just go back up north where I came from? Same reason as always, of course: money. Do you know any translators who get contracts for big television networks … and don't live in a major city? Didn't think so. I know, I know, with a good internet connection I could work from anywhere in the world. Too bad no one else gets it, especially those at the helm of the Reality Channel. Their excuse? The monthly charade known as our "team meeting." The coffee is awful, the agenda of scant concern to me. This definitely isn't where we decide which TV shows to purchase. And the texts I get to translate are invariably of the same abysmal quality. Let's just say compelling dialogue isn't high on the list of priorities. They invite me along so I can feel like "part of the team."

That's the official version, anyway. Since it's my first halfway decent job, I'm loath to complain. I didn't spend all these years studying to wait tables at a Normandin diner, the most exciting job on offer within thirty kilometres of Dupuis Creek last time I checked. I considered trying my luck as a drug dealer; as far as I can tell, it's both the most sought-after and the most lucrative career in the hole I grew up in. But when you go down that route, it doesn't take long before everyone knows who you are. Then they'll never leave you alone. I value my free time.

Unlike the rest of my university class, I never laboured under the delusion that I'd one day get the call to translate Donna Tartt or Chuck Palahniuk. Truth be told, though I like complaining about it, I actually enjoy my job. My work makes me laugh. It may not pay especially well, but as long as I make my deadlines and show up at meetings, they leave me alone. I guess at the interview they must have picked up on my fascination with sordid things. Not everyone gets off watching a perpetual loop of shows that work hard to strike the perfect balance between banal and pathetic. That's why it's called "reality," I guess.

So the French-speaking world has me to thank when they sit down to enjoy such marvels as *Get Thin and Get Rich*; *Shame on Me, Doctor!*; *Why Am I Gaining Weight?* (UK Edition); *Renovate Your Life*; *Crazy Screw-Ups*,

Surprise Birth!; *Ultimate Humiliation*; *Job Swap* (Australian Edition); *Babysitter Spy*; *Polygamous and Proud*; *36 Hours, No Sleep: Safari Edition*; *Better Living Through Surgery*; *The Torturers: Asia vs. America*; *Down Syndrome Heirs*; *Extreme World Tour* (Autistic Special); *Crazy Teenagers*; *Hoarding* (Season 5); *Animal Lovers*; and the list goes on.

Maybe one day they'll let me make my own show. It'll be something about morbidly obese women who don't know they're pregnant and have to swap husbands while renovating their houses to put them on the market. Don't worry, everyone will be under medical supervision. The show will be sponsored by a popular brand of ham or margarine, or maybe an over-the-counter heartburn medication. I just need to find the right title.

I'm hungry. There's nothing to eat. I need to go outside.

Why, you may ask, must I endure the indignity of roasting like a rotisserie chicken on the corner of a treeless street on this fine July 16? Why, to deposit a cheque at the bank, of course. Crossing this heat island is the final step before reaching the air-conditioned cell that houses the closest ATM. I can already picture the oily buttons, with the green "OK" worn away by thousands of greasy fingers indicating their agreement to the machine's statement.

My employer has arranged it so I am legally self-employed, which spares them the expense of an actual employee. To top it off, they insist on paying me with actual paper cheques, issued every two weeks. Hello, 1965.

The pictogram across the avenue is blinking white. I cross the street, fantasizing about the ice cube I'll melt on my neck once I get home. In the middle of the road I feel a hot wind, much hotter than the black asphalt, and hear a cacophony of engine sounds and honking. A black SUV turning the corner avoids crushing me by a matter of inches. The driver gives me the finger, then speeds off in a screech of burnt rubber. Bastard did it on purpose.

Usually drivers are satisfied to stomp on the accelerator after they've let a pedestrian cross. It's their charming little way of making it clear that we've wasted their precious time, since they have far more important places to go than we lowly walkers. They rarely go so far as to graze us. Just an angry squeal of tires and a jerky peel-out, though they're going to have to stop all over again in another 150 metres. But being grazed, with a middle finger to boot, that's new.

It scared me. The adrenalin hits, and I quake in fear as I watch the big vehicle speed off. I mentally note the licence plate number. The other pedestrians stare, feeling sorry for me or outraged by the incident. I shrug my shoulders. It's over. What else can I do? My supporters share my outrage and curse out the driver while I wait in line for the ATM. The air conditioning at the bank eventually calms me and my sympathizers down.

A few weeks go by. The incident is filed away along with all the others. 147 BTS. One more entry in my mental ledger.

Back at the beginning of my adult life, I was living with two friends in a student apartment, which is another way of saying an apartment for poor people. We eat a whole lot of pasta because we're too proud to go complaining to our parents about the monetary constraints of our new-found freedom. Noodles, coffee, weed: pretty much your typical student diet.

Our landlord stubbornly refuses to maintain his apartment building. Our landlord: the crazy old dude we pay rent to; the one who, no matter how many times we ask him, refuses to do anything about the sticky front door, or the two taps that drip relentlessly no matter how firmly we turn them off, or the mould slowly blooming on the bathroom walls, or the four missing window screens, or (and above all) the cold January wind slipping in through a crack between the floor and walls of our three-bedroom apartment.

We live on the third floor, between three layers of wall. Because, instead of taking the time to strip the internal walls down to the studs, some amateur-ass construction guys had the bright idea of just building new ones right over the old ones. We know that, in case you're wondering, because one night while drinking we slammed a door a little too hard. Through the hole we'd made, we could see the drywall of the previous wall underneath. Since we'd already gone that far, we broke through that layer of drywall, to the brick. Gus made a joke that you could hide a body between the walls. I laughed.

We like our apartment for the plain and simple reason that it's ours. By "we" I mean Gus, Simone, and I. Gus still has the body of a teenager: long arms and legs that have outgrown his torso. He's a nice guy, if a little full of himself sometimes. A sociology student, but we don't hold it against him since he makes great pesto. Gus works at a used book and record store, where he blows a third of his paycheque on dusty CDs and books. They pile up in stacks on the floor of his room, eighteen items high on average. (I never got out of the habit of counting stuff.) His organizational system isn't infallible, though. Gus is always surprised to discover that he has bought multiple copies of the same item. If it's something half-decent, and we happen to be around when he realizes, Simone or I will inherit the extra copy. At other times he forgets all about these moments of generosity. He'll go searching through our rooms, and sometimes he'll come across something he remembers buying. Then he'll accuse us of stealing his shit. Until we locate the other copy of the book or album tucked away at the bottom of a pile somewhere. Then all is forgiven.

Simone is Gus's cousin. She has no idea how to dye her hair properly. She's worried about burning her scalp with the lightening solution, so her hair always looks greasy, because the part that grows back is always a shade darker than the rest of her hair. But she's also a cheapskate, so there's no way she'd go to a hairdresser. Oh, and she makes her own clothes. Baggy sewn or knit ensembles that are far too fragile for our old washing machine. Simone washes everything by hand. Need I mention that she's not about to use the dryer? So her clothes are always stretched out on a drying rack in the corner of the kitchen. We don't have an exhaust fan over our stove, and our windows don't open in winter. So you can well imagine the smell of wet clothing, cooking, and cigarettes that constitutes our apartment's particular atmosphere.

Simone dreams of being a photographer, which is unfortunate since digital photography is poised to

OF VENGEANCE

annihilate that possibility. Especially since she's not overly endowed in the talent department. And it's not exactly easy to stand out today, when everyone spends all their time taking pictures. Her work looks pretty much like what anyone could do with a two-thousand-dollar camera.

Her parents support her; they're proud to have an artist in the family. She takes pictures of alleys, messy rooms (like our living room), that kind of thing. She also likes to create still lifes with naked people and standard embarrassing items: vibrators, pig's heads, money, blood. Simone's art practice involves frequent trips to the butcher shop. She doesn't have a lot of imagination. But then, who am I to judge? I'm just a two-bit translator.

Not to oversell myself; I'm actually a five-cent translator. See, at the time I'm writing about, we translators bill by the word. Five cents a word, in my case. I'm one of those people undercutting my fellow professionals, but what can I do? I have to pay my share of rent somehow, until I finally get the diploma declaring my fitness for the job I was already doing. In the meantime, I work for the kind of people who think it's a good idea to entrust their translation work to a college student. Most of my clients are travel agencies, beauty parlours, and car dealerships. I advertise my services on the bulletin boards at colleges and universities, and on a few other specialized websites. I also edit people's term papers, but that doesn't pay very well. Students are cheap. I live with Gus and Simone because I was the first person to answer their little ad. I took a trip with my parents to check out the city three weeks before class started, and that was when I saw the letter-sized sheet stapled to a hydro pole in front of the pub across from the college.

> Room Available. Apartment just shitty enough for a self-respecting student. 2 inbred unambitious roommates. No cat allergies.

Also on the poster: the price of the rent and a photo of a turkey. Typical Gus. His sense of humour is pretty off the wall. (He took the photo because Simone's an *Artiste*, so her work is too "important" to be subjected to a photocopier and the elements.) The bottom of the sheet was cut into strips with the phone number. I tore the whole sheet off the pole. This place had my name on it.

It turned out that there was no cat. They wrote that just for fun, or maybe to fuck with people. Simone believes you can't trust people who are allergic to animals, people who convert their unhappiness into psychosomatic symptoms. She also doesn't want anyone's hyperactive glands standing in her way should she ever want to adopt a kitten.

I have lots of great memories with Gus and Simone. Nights of drinking, doing hot knives, sex (not among roommates, though: they're cousins; and Gus isn't my type). No, I don't spend all my free time drowning pre-teens. I have my little habits, sure, but no murders since Fat Fiset. I'm in a dormant period. In hindsight I'd ascribe my passivity through those years to our favourite pastime: smoking a shit-ton of weed. Everybody knows that the herb saps your motivation. We'd get high before eating a meal. We'd get high before watching a movie. We'd get high before listening to music, and we'd get high before having a chat. We'd also get high before class. And after class. We'd get high before fucking. We'd get high with our morning coffee, with our evening noodles, and while taking a shower. Basically we'd get high before getting high.

Simone believes in cutting the filters for our joints out of materials with symbolic importance for us. My favourite is the student newspaper. Gus likes to work his way through all the funeral parlour bookmarks left over from his father's funeral. Simone is partial to marriage and birth announcements. They come from a huge family, so we can barely keep up. The little rectangles keep getting bigger and bigger, and we keep rolling tighter and tighter.

One of our genius ideas was our attempt to insulate the apartment. Most of the air currents were coming in from the street side, along the ground where the wall met the floor.

January 12: It's -14 degrees Celsius, -23 with the wind chill factor. We're freezing and the heater isn't equal to the task. So we smoke a joint and decide to take a trip to the hardware store.

We let a sympathetic father figure talk us into buying a can of spray-foam insulation. It's on sale for $9.99, which we can manage between the three of us. We opt not to buy the spray gun to apply it. Dad's annoyed, says that's a sure path to a half-ass job, which is, of course, precisely what we intend to do. We get home, smoke a little more reefer to get in the mood, and get down to work. Without the gadget to flatten the tube and extrude the yellow foam at a uniform rate, the result isn't pretty. Gus mans the foam while Simone and I provide running commentary. Eventually all the cracks appear to be nicely patched, and we're proud of ourselves. Just one hitch: it turns out we bought "expanding" foam, meaning its volume swells as it dries. We hadn't planned on quite so much expansion. The magic of chemistry!

The building structure has been creaking for a good three weeks now. And there's no question we've made matters worse since the apartment is no easier to heat than it was before our little renovation.

Two years later I inherited what was left in the tube of foam insulation when my friends moved out.

That infernal summer gave up the ghost early. The moment the heat wave relented, the days started getting shorter. The leaves changed colours, and I got back to my business. Long walks. Exploring.

I take a methodical approach: cover the entire area one street at a time, parallel arteries first, followed by perpendicular. I walk. I observe people and buildings. Note who has dogs or cats, which houses appear to be vacant, and which ones are full of people. I observe this ritual for weeks on end then move on to the next neighbourhood. I become a familiar figure, blend into the landscape. People grow accustomed to my presence. I become invisible. The street people start saying hi, and I smile back.

Invisibility is an art, a science, a way of life. There's nothing magical about what I do. It's basic psychology: know your environment. No one notices the people they see every day. Ordinary things don't make it through our mental filter. You also have to strike the perfect balance between pretty and ugly. People are fascinated by either end of the spectrum, which triggers a red light in their minds. I don't want to leave a scar in anyone's memory. I keep my eyes cast down. I don't go around dishing out smiles. I put on a gloomy face, walk calmly, tailor every movement to blend in to my surroundings. Beauty, like ugliness, attracts attention; it is therefore to be avoided at all costs.

For these outings, I dress unremarkably and style my hair just like every other woman my age. I steer clear of makeup. I wash with the mildest of soaps, free of perfume and friendly to both sensitive scalps and innocent bunnies. Products that won't give me cancer, certified by dermatologists the world over, approved by the most demanding of women. I choose a dish soap for people who are allergic to everything, those poor hypersensitive souls who faint if they walk too close to a dryer grate. I tell people that I, too, have sensitive skin. Who doesn't have sensitive skin these days? It's all the rage.

The best way to be invisible is to make sure no one notices you. People walk right by me on the sidewalk. I pass them on my bike; I jog right by. And on every one of these excursions, there's nothing about me that's interesting in the least.

Today's my lucky day. I've been exploring a new neighbourhood for a few weeks. Suddenly, there it is. Sleek, black, and silent. 147 BTS. I note the address. I come back several times. I'm carefully plotting my next move.

I conduct a few tests, one of the benefits of living alone.

Then, one rainy night (no one goes out running on rainy nights in November), I take the tube of insulating foam with me. First I carefully wash the can in the sink (for fingerprints, you never know). I put on gloves. I take my umbrella. The aerosol can is in a plastic bag in my big satchel.

I go out and walk to the address. It takes precisely two hours and forty-seven minutes. The SUV is there, gleaming like a killer whale. I fill the exhaust pipe with insulating foam. Not too much, just enough to block the pipe once it dries. I put the can back in the bag and leave again. It's dark and deadly still. I'm the only one on the road. It's a residential neighbourhood, there are no cameras, and no one would leave their dog outside in weather like this.

It takes another three hours to walk back. It's 2:00 a.m. The carpeting and ceilings welcome me home with their exquisite aroma of old ashtray. And that's the end of the story. I'll never know what happened with the SUV. I'm not stupid enough to stand around waiting to find out.

I've developed a bit of a habit. At first I thought about using a potato, but I hate the idea of wasting food. And there was always the chance that when the car started the potato might shoot out like a cannonball. The last thing I wanted was collateral victims. Trust me, it happens; I've tried it before. The summer we weren't allowed to play outside I stole a potato from my mom. It ended up in the neighbour's exhaust pipe. Just a test. He started his car: the potato was catapulted against the wall of his house. Instant mashed potatoes. My neighbour never noticed a thing.

Another option would be a good old-fashioned tire slashing, but that's too risky for my liking. Blades have never been my thing. I'm also scared of the tire exploding, even if my rational mind knows it can't happen. Plus the idea feels uninspired since I've seen it before, in a Kundera novel where one of the characters gets off on randomly attacking car tires along his jogging route. Not to mention that used tires have to be disposed of, which causes a lot of pollution. At least mufflers get recycled. There are armies of scrap metal guys dedicating their lives to recycling metal.

Over the following months I targeted a fish shop, a print shop, a caterer, a general contractor, and a parachute school. Always for the same reason: their vehicles were driven by people who consistently committed basic infractions. Excessive speeding, failure to stop for pedestrians, sound pollution, general boorishness.

What these people forget is that their business name is written on their vehicle in eighteen-inch letters. Anyone with a modicum of determination can easily find their address, and from there it's no problem at all to fill a few exhaust pipes with expanding foam. Much easier than finding an unmarked vehicle from only a licence plate number.

Like with my asshat SUV-driver, I never saw what came of these misdemeanours. I once went so far as to scope out one of the businesses a bit, but apart from a few vehicles that seemed to be out of commission for a few weeks, I saw no tangible effects.

I threw the empty can in a dumpster seven blocks north of my apartment the day before July 1, moving day all over Quebec and the biggest garbage day of the year. Oh, and Canada Day. I realized I was going about this the wrong way. If there's one thing I hate more than dangerous drivers and pollution, it's waste. And I'd come to the conclusion that vandalism is a form of waste. So it was time to move on. We've all done things we aren't proud of.

I keep memorizing licence plate numbers, though, whenever I witness a driver endangering the public, out of force of habit.

4

Early Days

Other than the potato incident, the months following my manslaughter were relatively uneventful. I was on my guard. I knew that one fine morning I'd be happily drinking my Quik and watching the morning show on TV when the police kicked in the door, broke the kitchen window, and smashed my dad's head against the counter, right next to our toaster. They'd pin me down and read me my rights. My mom would let out a few sobs, and I'd remain silent, save to ask for a lawyer. I'd plead not guilty. I'd tell them I had been somewhere else. I'd argue that in such a short time there was no way I could have picked enough strawberries for my mom to make a pie. We're talking tiny wild strawberries, your Honour, they're nothing like the big hothouse berries we're used to seeing.

My lack of preparation has left me with a half-ass alibi. I'll never make this mistake again; it's far too stressful.

When my family moves, things calm down in my head. I'm increasingly able to convince myself that no one will ever find out. Ever. No one saw. No one can read my thoughts. Fiset is six feet underground, and I'm still here, out in the big wide world, biding my time in a packed, stifling classroom. The teacher is soldiering on with her explanation of the importance of budgeting. Since every one of her students is convinced they're going to be millionaires, she doesn't make much headway. Everything is as it should be. At that very moment, not a single person is thinking about me. No one suspects me. "How much does a smoker, who smokes one pack a day at $7.95 each, spend on cigarettes in a year? What else could that person do with that amount of money?" This teacher is after my own heart.

The thing about secrets is they wear you down. I'd never really understood when people described something as a "heavy weight to bear." It's not that I feel guilty, but it's hard not being able to brag about it to anyone. So I do my best to forget the whole thing.

My teenage years have been mostly smooth sailing up to now. Like a lot of people my age, I have no doubt that I am the very centre of the universe, and no one else has anything better to do than spy on my every word and action, judge my appearance, and talk behind my back. My rational mind may understand that the world doesn't work that way, but this exaggerated sense of my own importance will take years to fade. Just because you're paranoid doesn't mean they're not after you.

My parents are the only people I still spend time with who remember what I was like at that age — people whose blind love and fundamental goodness prevents them from seeing the perfectly ordinary evil brewing in their daughter. This is my favourite explanation. There's another, simpler one, though: I'm good at hiding who I really am. It's one of my greatest strengths, one I've been perfecting since I was a child. For example, even today my dad has no idea that his lawn mower fell prey to an act of sabotage. With all the insight of a ten-year-old, I was violently opposed to the biweekly massacre of the wildflowers that grew on our lawn. They'd worked so hard to grow back, overcoming the colonizing grass and the barbecue, pollution, and adversity of their ecosystem. I wouldn't have phrased it quite like that back then, of course, but I was already driven by the same rage and feelings of powerlessness as today.

My dad also had no idea that the people he hired to fix his lawn mower were a bunch of incompetents. All they had to do was tighten three bolts, and the machine would have been good as new. Unless by loosening those three bolts I'd done irreparable damage to the motor, that is. Either way, our lawn mower was never the same again. Even after he had it repaired, the blades would regularly jam, only to come unstuck a few feet farther on. After he was done mowing, my dad would have to level out a bunch of uneven spots on the lawn with the Weed Eater. The problem was never quite bad enough to justify buying a new mower, though. All I'd managed to do was suck out all the joy my father once got from mowing the lawn.

After we move, time passes and I get better at dissembling my emotions. I stop shaking when I make one of my "plays." I learn to lie without shifting on my feet. I begin constantly observing others. I try out a few innocent little experiments, like switching the positions of objects and observing how their owners react. I'm a snoop. I know who has something to hide; or, rather, I know who's stupid enough to leave blackmailable items lying around where I can find them. You have to understand that the dominant emotion throughout my teenage years was boredom. An all-pervasive ennui that lasted four or five years, leaving me feeling completely detached, as if what other people did scarcely affected me. *Who are these people?* I wondered. *Do they really deserve to live?*

The advantage of not knowing anyone is that it goes both ways: no one knows you either. So I didn't have to be the same person I was before. I was free to be whomever I wanted to be. My parents loved me unconditionally and were far too absorbed in their daily routine to notice any changes. All I had to do was take care not to disappoint them. Friends? They were pretty much nonexistent during those years. The few I had managed to make were left behind along with our old home. They've grown hazy in my memory. Mine was the euphoric state of the happy few who get the opportunity to reinvent themselves. I had a few humdrum acquaintances, people I hung out with now and then but wouldn't call friends. People left me alone. People are perceptive like that, even kids. Survival is an inborn human instinct.

I remember very little of my teenage years. The more time passes, the more I have trouble distinguishing between real and imaginary events. Like everyone else, I had a miserable adolescence. Not just because of the boredom, but also for the lack of clear answers. I couldn't exactly go around asking people to explain why life was worth living. That would have raised suspicions. So I put the question aside, on grounds of reasonable doubt. And it's a good thing I did since nowadays I can barely remember those years. Definitely nothing happened to justify the effort of covering my tracks after a major crime. In other words, I decreed that all teenagers were stupid and everyone deserves to be cut a little slack.

I can summon up a few names from those days: Roy and Carol Anne, Eva, Stephanie, and Hurteau and Frosty. If I really pushed myself, I could probably list a few more, but for the most part those were my "dog years." I spent more time with animals than with people. None of these people really deserve to be punished. I'm not one of those pathetic individuals who never gets over their horrible childhood and spends years cultivating revenge fantasies, only to finally go after the little local bully with a machete or turn them down for a job. I'd probably be perfectly happy to read their names in a story of a sex scandal involving farm animals, but mostly just because that's my kind of news story, no matter who gets caught with their pants down. When I seek vengeance, it's rarely for a crime against my own person.

I guess what I'm saying is that Fiset didn't deserve to die. At least, not right away. It was an accident. Every murder leaves its mark, scars a soul; mine will never be unblemished again. So you have to be careful not to waste your opportunities. But at the same time, what's done is done; there's no going back. At least, when I see what happened to Fiset's big brother, who's in prison for rape, I figure that what I did gave Fiset the younger an easy out. He'll live on in memory as a saint. Death is cleansing. It makes us better people than we actually were. People miss you. Trust me, I know, since every single one of my "projects" after Fiset concerned a terrible person who richly deserved their fate. And yet I haven't read a single bad word about them after they were eliminated.

But for now, I'm a regular teenager, busy learning a number of things I'll put to use later, about people who commit unpardonable acts. When a chasm appears, we grow stronger so we can leap over it. On one side, there you are; on the other, the land we cannot quite reach. Neverland.

There's just one way across: you have to learn to fly. Keep your joyful thoughts to yourself, learn doublethink, and dig a trench between who you actually are and the person you think you are. Olympic athletes must use techniques like this, holding on to their dreams of glory like climbers grasping ropes in their bloody palms as they hang over the side of a mountain. They just soldier on despite their injuries, stillborn social lives, coaches committing unspeakable acts on road trips, crazy parents living out lost dreams through their children. Because giving up while you're flying full-speed ahead would mean falling to your death in the blinding light of the camera flashes.

———

My list of names does bring a few stories to mind. It's all I've really got, for those years.

Roy and Carol Anne

I never really learned who Roy was, just saw his name carved with an X-acto blade into the arm of the girl sitting to the right of me in class. Her name was Carol Anne — I remember because it reminded me of *Poltergeist*. "Do not go into the light, Carol Anne!" Aside from her name, I don't think Carol Anne had anything in common with the pretty blond kid in the movie. Our Carol Anne had a big round face, a nose covered in blackheads, and thick black hair. She gave off that distinct odour of cigarettes and fabric softener I've always associated with poverty.

Carol Anne was part of a mysterious group of kids I never really talked to. Most of them had failed at least one grade. They spent recess in a corner of the schoolyard known as the Smoke Pit, an area around one hundred square feet where smoking was tolerated. This was back when anyone could buy smokes, even children, a bygone era that wasn't actually so long ago. The school rule was that anyone who wanted to smoke could, but only in the designated area. This, of course, meant that only certain people could actually smoke at school since the Pit was contested territory. Other smokers had to slip off the school grounds or face the consequences. When Carol Anne walked by you between the rows of desks in class, it smelled as if someone had emptied an ashtray while waving a sheet of Bounce in the air. And Carol Anne had asthma. Her gentle wheezing was the soundtrack to grade nine. She was permanently congested, and kept her mouth open throughout the entire process of carving Roy's name into her arm. I could gauge the intensity of her pain by the cadence of her wheezing, which sped up as she dug the blade deeper into her flesh.

With a name like his, Roy could only ever be an object of mockery, and the subject of all kinds of speculation. The whole class knew what Carol Anne was up to with the knife, including the teacher. Why didn't she do anything about it? Was it a sense of decorum, or an aversion to looking at ugly people long enough for the focus to take? With her oily hair, shiny nose, and open mouth, Carol Anne was repulsive. She was surrounded by a personal magnetic field that warped your senses. She could have built a bomb right in her school desk, and no one would have stopped her.

Now she's a pharmacist. I know because she sent me a Facebook friend request a few years ago. I accepted. She posts a random combination of PharmaSave Halloween specials, pictures of her new house, and lamentations over her repeated miscarriages. *Marie-Lilou's little sister has joined the other angels in heaven today. I'm writing this here so I won't have to answer everyone's questions. Please give us some time to grieve* … blah blah blah. It took every ounce of my willpower to refrain from posting that she should look on the bright side: at least we have five days left to print photos in-store for just ten cents a shot.

What I'd really love to ask Carol Anne is whether she used a laser to remove her scars. But I don't dare. There's no Roy in her Facebook friends, and she has tons of friends. Some people friend the entire world when they start a business, gathering up all the contacts they've ever crossed paths with in the hope of giving their sales a boost. Other people do it for no discernible reason.

Eva

I used to enjoy observing Eva, who was known as a bit of a bozo. There was nothing mean about it. Staring at her was like staring at a baby or at a fire burning in the grate; there was no need to be discreet. She barely seemed to notice. And we all liked Eva. One sunny morning, in an attempt to wake us up and make us feel a little bit guilty for not paying attention, our chemistry teacher made a joke: "C'mon, I walked through ten feet of snow to be here today." And good old Eva answered, "What do you mean? It's a hot sunny day!" Classic Eva.

So in physics one time, to demonstrate the laws of electrical conductivity, our teacher brought in a little machine consisting of a light bulb and a crank. To light up the bulb, you turned the crank and positioned your finger so it could conduct the charge. The teacher asked the class if anyone wanted to give it a try. When Eva volunteered, someone yelled out: "Not sure it's gonna light up." Laughter all around. This apparent cruelty concealed the fact that we would all have lined up in front of Eva to serve as a human shield. She somehow brought out the noblest in our nature, represented everyone's inner child. Car accident four years ago; killed instantly. I read it on Carol Anne's wall.

Stephanie

If Eva was the class bozo, Stephanie was the school slut. Or at least that's what people said. It wasn't true. Our school was a small one, barely three classes per grade. Everyone knew each other and rumours spread fast. People used to say the only thing in town that hadn't hit Steph was the train. I thought she was nice. I used to wonder why the other girls resented her so much. I have a theory: Stephanie was really pretty and had huge breasts, which cast a shadow over their own efforts to seduce the boys.

She just couldn't win, at least when it came to getting some respect. The guys would say all kinds of dirty shit about her; the girls' cruelty was more finely honed. But Steph kept her spirits up. She must not have known what people said about her. What strikes me when I remember Stephanie is how beauty and desire are at once sources of power and Pandora's boxes of problems. She's one of the few people I watched really closely during high school. You couldn't take your eyes off her. I was just as fascinated as everyone else.

I realized that Stephanie incarnated the opposite of invisibility, a quality I've always viewed as a basic asset to my mission. Her every movement was closely watched by all, including the teachers, especially the male teachers. They must have had to steel themselves by reciting key paragraphs of the Criminal Code every time she bent over to tie her shoes. Steph got pregnant and dropped out of college, and then got a full-time restaurant job. I heard it from my mom.

Hurteau and Frosty

Another rumour going around high school was that Hurteau did hard drugs. Heroin. The truth was his backpack contained nothing more illicit than a tube of cortisone cream. He preferred to have everyone believe he was a drug addict than admit that the little patches around his elbows were eczema. The ravages of skin disease look nothing like track marks, but at my school no one was too scrupulous about that kind of detail.

Hurteau's parents owned the snack bar in the mall. Dave (for that was his first name) worked there. He always smelled like fries, which always made me hungry. Hurteau also kept a diary: a pile of loose-leaf folded in quarters, so worn that the paper had taken on the texture of flannel. The sheets would tear when I unfolded them to read. He didn't write anything all that interesting, just a few notes on the porn flicks he watched with Frosty, and a few vaguely obscene drawings featuring Stephanie or the school social worker.

Frosty was Dave Hurteau's best friend, and vice versa. We called him Frosty for obvious reasons. He used to joke around, said "getting frosted" brought out his true personality. He was super good-looking. At first no one really noticed Frosty. His features were pretty standard, but everything about him was perfect. He had great arms, beautiful hands, a nice neck, a straight back, a tight ass, and muscular legs. A lot of young men, especially at that age, have the lower body of a chicken, but not Frosty. Good genes. That guy had a hearty laugh and a firm erection. He slept well at night. And he was funny. He smelled like melted butter; it was especially noticeable when he hadn't showered for a few days. To this day I think about those two every time I go into a greasy spoon for breakfast.

Hurteau and Frosty were the main people I hung out with in high school. They must have put up with me because I was the only girl who gave them the time of day. My own life didn't interest them much. Their main concerns were whether I was holding any weed, whether they could smoke it with me, and whether the G spot actually existed. Our favourite thing to do was watch *The Simpsons* while eating jujubes and waiting for the knives on the stove to turn red. Oh, and sex, of course. What self-respecting teenager would pass up the chance? I know human relationships can offer much more complex joys, but that would have required putting in far more energy than I was getting out of it. Those two took off for California right after high school. Made a fortune when medical marijuana was legalized. I go visit them every couple years. We talk about the good old days and tell the same old stories, like the time Frosty was so fast asleep that the pool of drool on his desk started dripping onto the classroom floor.

5

Good Dogs

The problem with most people is they never shut up. They're constantly *communicating*, forever shoving their noses in your business. They're hard to keep in check. They never stop inventing scenarios and harbouring suspicions. They take wrong turns. They're hard to figure out. They're unpredictable. They lie. They're terrible actors. They self-destruct. They're cruel.

For all these reasons, I far prefer animals. At least with them you know where you stand. Some even have better hygiene than humans. And with animals, no matter what happens to them, the only way they can give you an opinion is with a display of raw emotion. You'll never know if something happened to your animal unless it's struck by a feeling of raw terror. So I've begun getting up at the crack of dawn, especially in summer when the sun rises early. Where I live, light starts creeping over the horizon around three in the morning in mid-June. The few people who do cross your path are too sleepy or intoxicated to care what you're up to at such an ungodly hour. Outside of the city all you hear are the sounds of nature: birds, the wind, insects, rain. I can sometimes imagine that I'm all alone in the world.

It's an old habit, going all the way back to my child-hood when I was first old enough to unlock the front door on my own. On weekend mornings my parents stay in bed, on principle. Even if they actually wake up at the same time as during the week, sleeping in is a sacred ritual, and they stay in their room until mid-morning. That's why, all through childhood, most of my Saturday morning expeditions went unnoticed. When I did get "caught," I was all innocence: riding my trike in the driveway, watching snails in the garden, oh, and that one aborted mission when they caught me in the midst of preparations, stuffing cookies into my little backpack. I always bring cookies. Still one of my favourite provisions.

I discovered that an effective trick to avoid getting caught was to turn the TV to the kids' channel. The hard part was finding the right volume. Since it was usually too early for me to be up, it had to be quiet enough not to wake up my parents, but loud enough for them to hear once they did wake up. The perfect level, on our old grey Hitachi, was six green bars out of fifteen. There was always the risk of failing to turn the volume down in time, since my dad liked to watch sports at full blast, and the previous setting would be stored when I turned the TV back on the next day. The solution was to smother the TV speakers with a cushion while I made the adjustment. Later, when I had the excuse of being a teenager, since all teenagers like to sleep in, I would sneak back in through my window around 8:00 or 9:00 a.m. If I went out at 3:00 a.m., that left six hours for my unsupervised outing. Leave nothing to chance, minimize risk, create optimal conditions: just as I always brought cookies with me, I always followed these ground rules.

In the beginning I did little more than explore the surroundings of the house: the street, the lawn, the strip of forest. I ran with the neighbourhood cats. To this day, I envy those cats their discretion and heightened senses. They don't trust me, and I respect that, even if it makes me a little sad. Cats are even less predictable than humans, but I can ignore them if I want. No one trusts cats. They're known for being undependable. To the best of my knowledge, no murderer has ever been caught because of a cat. In danger? Don't expect your cat to warn you. Lost? Too bad, they can't track you. What cats are good at is sitting back and observing in silence.

Next I got into dogs. The ones that were tied up, not going anywhere. It took a while for me to approach them since barking scared me. There was Theodore, the neighbours' German shepherd, who'd get excited the moment I got close. He'd bark, yank on his chain, and rouse the entire street. When I understood that all I had to do to shut him up was go over and say hi, things got much more straightforward. The ideal scenario was for me to already be beside him when he became aware of my presence so the idea of barking wouldn't even enter his mind. Because at the time of day I was out and about, Theo would be sleeping. I'd wake him by dropping the leftovers from last night's dinner right under his nose. We got to be good pals. After I moved, I had to walk 95 minutes (in summer) and 105 (in winter), through the forest, to go see my old friend.

Making friends with dogs became a game to me. I challenged myself to get in tight with the mangiest mutts in the neighbourhood, and the most vicious ones as well. The louder their bark and the more they bared their fangs, the better. The ones whose owners never took them for walks. I'd watch the shows about famous dog trainers on TV and try out their techniques. Most didn't work, but feeding them did. Between ages nine and seventeen, almost my entire allowance went to dog treats. I'd go to the next town over to make my purchases (seventy-eight minutes on foot; twenty-four by bike). I liked to be discreet.

I started keeping to the background. I'd set up on the edge of someone's yard, somewhere humans couldn't see me. I liked properties near the forest so I could go home along paths and avoid the streets. I wore warm, dark-coloured clothing. Rainy days were best. The relaxing ambient sound of misty raindrops. The powerful smell of wet plants. There's a lovely, sadly little-known word for this phenomenon: petrichor. People need to get outside a little more.

Water dissolves impurities and washes all it touches clean. And rain also cuts down on the number of people out.

I'd toss the dog a few morsels, watch it eat, and then start again. Some were kept on short leashes by their owners; others would wind their chains around their doghouse or a tree, and then couldn't figure out how to untangle themselves. They'd end up half-strangled. I'd spend several hours with each animal, very early in the morning. I'd focus on the ones that barked lots since the neighbours would have been desensitized to the barking and stopped paying attention. Then I'd give the dog some time to get used to my presence. Some took a few sessions, but most dogs accepted me after just one or two. I'd sit down close, give them some food and water, speak softly to them. I'd pet them a little, too, even though most were pretty gross. It's true what the dog trainers say: there are no bad dogs, just bad owners.

Spending so much time with dogs taught me to cultivate patience. I also learned to observe people carefully. I'd choose a patch of ground that wasn't covered in dog shit and take a seat. Once a dog accepted me, I was free to approach the house and peer through the windows. I'd watch the sun rise from the patio. Unplug the pool pumps, to hear better. And I'd play little tricks, nothing serious. Swap dogs. I'd secretly bought a leash, and I kept it on a nail I'd hammered in under our balcony for that purpose. I'd collect one dog, then tie it somewhere next to the spot where I planned to pick up the other one. I couldn't just do the exchange right on the spot since you never know how two dogs meeting each other for the first time are going to react. Then I'd take the second dog to the first one's home and tie it up, and tie the first one in the usual spot of the second. It caused a lot of confusion.

This stopped making me laugh once I realized it was harmful to the dogs. Their behaviour scared people. They would have to be dominated and taken home by force. It wasn't a pretty sight. Often once they got home they'd be punished, as if it were their fault. I'd come back and apologize. They never held grudges. But my stratagem wasn't just hurting the dogs; it was also attracting attention. So I went back to walking my canine friends in secret. I'd get started very early in the morning or on days when we didn't have school but the adults still had to work. It was easier in summer, but I tried to keep up my routine all year long. In winter I preferred snowy days, since the newly fallen flakes would cover my tracks. Your eyes get used to the dark, especially when there's moonlight. And you can hear better when it's very cold out.

The dogs and I would go walking through the forests. I'd throw sticks, but I never taught them to bring them back to me. Some did it anyway. Natural fetchers. But I had no wish to train them. They already had enough troubles in their miserable lives without my adding to them. They followed me anyway.

At the height of my dog years, I had a rota of seven dogs I'd take for walks. One every day. It was exhausting. I was barely getting any sleep. The hardest part was bringing them back and tying them up again while they wagged their tails. I had a whole bunch of excuses ready, in case I got caught. "I was just passing by because I'm a mushroom picker." "I saw a jackrabbit on your lawn." "Your dog got off its leash." But it only happened once, while I was tying a little mutt up to his pole. His owner came out in a yellow velour bathrobe.

"Hey, little girl. What are you doing?"

"Your dog got all wrapped around his stick. I wanted to give him a little room."

Slipping a little truth in makes your lie more persuasive. I took off without waiting for the guy to answer. I could picture him, though, standing there in the door, too lazy to get to the bottom of the story. The sad part is I had to stop walking that dog. I had a plan for a few others, but I had to put it on hold a few months to give the guy time to forget what had happened. You can never be too careful.

I had a lot of time to think, out walking strangers' dogs, all alone in the middle of nature. What was I to do? Kill the owners? They deserved it for treating good animals the way they did. But then what would happen? The dogs would be sent to the pound and be put down. Was the risk of being caught, and all the work that went into planning a murder, really worth it when the outcome would be an animal's death? Wouldn't it make more sense just to kill the dog right off the bat and put it out of its misery?

Dogs live in the present. When they were out with me, happily jogging alongside me with their snouts up in the breeze, neither past nor future meant a thing to them. I tried applying their teachings to my own life. I experienced moments of grace. I tried to decide when the time was right, but couldn't settle on a definition of happiness.

If I killed myself, I'd stop gathering new experiences. Sure, I'd have no more worries, but that wasn't a strong enough assurance to convince me to pull the plug. I still had things to accomplish. Like saving Pete. I never found out his real name. I just called him Pete after a character on a TV show. I liked the slightly exotic sound, the vague connotation of rebellion. Keep in mind that, at that point, the biggest city I'd ever seen was La Tuque, Quebec.

Poor Pete was always out on his metal chain, summer and winter. He had a wooden doghouse meant to protect him from the elements, but it did nothing to keep him from freezing in winter and roasting in summer. He slept on the ground. He didn't even have a blanket.

Pete was a big ol' mutt, a hell of a barker, and a real foul smeller. He must have been part Lab and part German shepherd, with two or three other breeds thrown in for good measure. It was February, and the entire area around his doghouse was unusable, covered in piles of frozen piss and shit. He must have been chained up there for months. His paws were covered in a half-inch of ice, and the skin around his claws cracked. He had enough to eat, but that was surely cold comfort. I knew he'd be in agony when it warmed up and his paws thawed out. I couldn't do it at his home; it was too delicate an operation. So I took Pete into our garage one Wednesday morning during school holidays. My parents were at work. Since their respective offices were practically next door to each other, they drove together in my mom's car. My dad's is a "collector's item," far too sensitive to expose to winter conditions. It had a reserved spot in the garage. My mom and I thought the car was ridiculous, but as she liked to say, you have to choose your battles. The dog spent three days in the garage. I had to move him at one point because the smell got too strong. Apart from eating and doing a little moaning because his paws were killing him, all he could do was sleep. Pete even had the decency to go to the bathroom on the cement floor instead of the back seat of the Toyota Cressida. He didn't even yap when my parents came home the first night or the next night. That surprised me. I'd resigned myself to having to explain what a dog was doing in our garage and concocted a story about finding a stray. We set off very early Saturday morning, around 6:00 a.m. We walked for a long time. It was a beautiful day: the sun in the sky, the snow melting. It smelled like spring. The plan was to take him out to Saint-Bouvier, a village fifteen kilometres from our house. I'd written a letter just in case I didn't manage to find a place to leave Pete. I had to make sure he'd be welcomed home if I had to take him back. I didn't exactly expect the owners to kill the fatted calf, but I was going to make it clear they had to let their dog in when it got below −15 degrees Celsius. I'd traced the letters with a stencil, which I hated because it made me look amateurish, childish. Cutting words out of the newspaper would have had the opposite effect, though: too scary, like in movies about psycho killers. They'd call the police. Plus, newspaper collages took way too long. I'd run the risk of my parents discovering my pile of paper scraps.

But I really didn't want to have to use the stencilled letter.

In the end, I handed Pete over to a couple in their thirties who were in the area to do some skiing. They had matching fluorescent pink headbands, and their noses were slathered in thick coatings of sunscreen. I said: "Here, I'm giving you my dog. My dad wanted to take him to the SPCA, but they'll put him down for sure because he's too old. He loves chicken. Don't give him chocolate because it can kill him. He's good with kids. His name is Pete."

Pete fell asleep next to their cooler, and they took it as a sign. I never found out what happened to him.

With the Rivards' dog, things didn't go quite so smoothly. He started running down the road because he saw a chipmunk. We hadn't even gone three kilometres. My plan was to see if I could leave him at the waterslides. I would have liked to find that dog a cute little family so he could have lived out his days in Brossard, or Jonquière, or maybe even Ontario, why not? He was a big black dog, sort of like a retriever but a little smarter and a lot furrier.

He ran away, though, and never came back. I hope he survived. I like to imagine him out chasing wolves. Before he disappeared, he used to be a loud barker. You could hear him all over the village, especially at night. Wherever he is now, let's hope he doesn't have to cry out for help anymore.

6

Big City

When I am plagued by doubt, I cheer myself up with the thought that for every wrong decision I've made, there exists a parallel universe where I made the right one. There's even a perfect universe out there where I'm a perfectly good person, spreading infinite tenderness all around me. I'm another person, anyone but that cruel, vengeful, cold-blooded killer on a vendetta for lost causes. My bravest actions aren't breaking laws but having the courage to tell the people close to me that I love them, each and every day. In this perfect world I harbour only pure, benevolent feelings for everyone, like the sense of marvel a mother has bringing her newborn to her breast, feeling the warm weight of the child in her arms and her little heart beating fast, fast, fast. It's not impossible. Just like there's a statistical possibility that you could walk through your living room wall, since everyone knows it's made of individual atoms and molecules with space between them.

One memory that will always epitomize my new life in the big city: the old man who didn't bother to pick up his dog's turds. It wasn't something I'd ever thought about before because where I come from, there's enough nature around to absorb the excreta of every living thing.

But sidewalks don't work that way. You don't exactly have to be a dog owner to wrap your head around the concept.

I'm not even on the lookout for a project — just drinking coffee and staring into space when he appears, right in front of my window, dragging a curly-haired mutt with yellow teeth and enough fur to obstruct his vision. The dog does his business, and then off they go, beast and master, leaving little balls of shit to dry right next to the back wheel of Gus's bike.

May as well just paint a target on his forehead.

I follow this pair around for two weeks. Twice a day they leave the big brown building they live in, three blocks down. A co-op or social housing, maybe. Hard to tell who exactly qualified for a spot: there are old people, obese people in wheelchairs, older women whose breasts sag down to their stomachs, all greeting each other in a hail of obscenity as they water their geraniums. No kids though. It's a brown ten-storey building with tiny windows, cluttered balconies, and a rotating collection of trash and broken crap that the garbage collectors could never quite get to the bottom of.

Our man lives in apartment 416. He has dubious hygiene, lots of free time, and a belaboured gait I first ascribe to athlete's foot and later decide must be rheumatism or an arthritic hip. While I'm at it, I diagnose early-stage emphysema and a lung tumour. No one can cough quite that way without a severe health problem. It's a scraping, greasy cough that turns my stomach, and his as well. I almost regret deciding on this zombie since now I'm stuck breathing in his vapour trail. Every new smoke he lights up triggers a fresh coughing fit that lasts several minutes, during which he repeatedly hacks up globs of phlegm from the inner reaches of his throat.

The man looks fairly old, but there's no easy way to determine his exact age. I've read that smoking constricts the blood vessels in the face, killing them at the surface. It deprives the outer layers of the epidermis of oxygen and essential nutrients, and premature aging sets in. He's a lovely specimen, with a grey face and hollowed-out cheeks. He shifts his dentures left to right when he finally stops coughing.

His sleeves and fingers are turning yellow, just like his dog's coat. Poor animal. He'll end up in the gas chamber of some shelter once his master's gone. It'll be a matter of months.

The man's radio is so loud you can hear it across the alley. I could have tracked him with a military band and he wouldn't have noticed. A nice easy play for me, to get back in practice.

On the last day I pick up his dog shit behind him. There's a lot of it. For such a tiny yapper, this dog shits as much as a grown man. I place his deposits in thin pink paper, which I seal at the edges with a lovely velveteen ribbon purchased in a store in another neighbourhood.

I enclose my fragile package in two layers of bubble-wrap then fasten the whole thing with a lot of tape to make it impossible to take anything out without cutting right into the bubble-wrap. There's no way to open this package and see what's inside without slicing through the pink paper.

Our kitchen reeks. I say that I stepped in dog shit and had to wash my shoes. Gus notes that there was shit on his bike last week, too. He's a week off, but I let it slide. I guess bending over would be too much pain and suffering for mister my-dog-shits-all-over-the-place-and-I-don't-care, but my tracking efforts have been enough to overcome all my scruples. The guy doesn't bother to pick anything up, or even to guide his animal off the beaten path to do its filthy business. When they take their daily walk, they leave little gifts in the middle of playgrounds and along the paths through the park. This guy clearly doesn't have one iota of respect for the society that has seen fit to subsidize his housing. Every day the dog soils places where hundreds of people — children mostly — walk and play. If only he'd spared Gus's bike.

I wrap up my little package like a precious gift. It's pretty heavy, which will help sustain the illusion. I throw in a couple biodegradable dog-shit bags, to point my old friend in the right direction. Once the mail carrier goes by, I'll place it in his mailbox with a little note.

To the resident of #416, with thanks!
From the neighbourhood.

I stick around to watch from a distance, blending into the surroundings. My victim usually gets back from his stroll at 11 a.m., around forty minutes after the mail arrives. There's always the risk that someone will steal a package, but this one ends up in its rightful owner's hands. The dog is sniffing around, visibly excited. They go inside. Mission accomplished.

Now the man knows he's being watched. A juvenile effort, admittedly, but enough to shake me out of my torpor. I realize that living with other people is getting in the way of my hobby. Now I'm ready to get back into it in earnest.

During that sticky summer, boiling away in my chicken coop of an apartment, I spend some time assessing my situation and realize it's not exactly dire. Despite its many drawbacks, my apartment has a tactically valuable view that doesn't fail to impress. I live on the fifth floor. The elevator is permanently out of order, but that just helps me keep in shape. Once we rip out the carpet, the ashtray smell finally goes away. I eventually get used to the heat.

In an attempt to cool down, I discover that I can hang out on the roof of the apartment. The door to get up there is locked, but I try picking the lock with a credit card, just like in the movies. Amazingly, it works.

I practise on the bathroom door, which has a similar mechanism. I try a range of different cards: credit cards, loyalty cards, hospital cards, licences, ATM cards, health insurance — even my library card. I also give my cousin's business card a shot. She made it when she opened a catering business for kids' birthday parties, before she began popping out her own brood and scuttled the venture. The card stock isn't stiff enough. I cut out a rectangle from a plastic pop bottle, a trick I picked up online. I use the two litres of pop to clean the toilet, another pearl of internet wisdom. No wonder our poutines are so easy to digest when we wash them down with such a corrosive liquid. The plastic rectangle works, but the technique lacks finesse. And I lose my deposit. I'm also a firm believer in always using tools designed for another purpose, which helps conceal their secondary usage. A curious person might ask questions about the contents of my recycling bin.

The gift card from the chain bookstore appears to be the best option. This Christmas gift from my uncle paid for a volume on survivalism. The ideal combination of flexibility and stiffness. I demagnetize it with fridge magnets, in case I drop it on the other side of the door without succeeding in opening it.

Even if it's against building rules, anyone who sees you heading onto the roof with a guitar case tends to give you the benefit of the doubt. It's a charmingly rebellious, even romantic act. But that's no reason to let myself get caught. The guitar case is an excuse. A security measure. When people think they know what you're up to, they stop asking questions.

What you need is an item — like my guitar case — that repels people just enough to make them look away so they don't notice where you're going. A little sleight of hand to occupy their minds.

I sand down the guitar case until it looks worn out, apply a light coating of glue, sprinkle on dirt and dust, and use black matte paint on any areas that still appear a little too shiny. I also make sure it doesn't smell.

I dig out the inside, removing the thin layer of foam designed to protect the instrument. The space I save will let me fit in both my little guitar and my gun snugly enough so neither will move or get scratched up. The end result is a somewhat bizarre case, dirty and worn out as if it had been lugged around the world by a starving artist. It embodies every cliché about penniless, dirty, and wonderfully inoffensive musicians with their cases open on the sidewalk, singing for their supper.

This guitar case is the most innocuous thing in the world. Like me, when I pay attention. People love music. They find musicians intriguing. They want to see them play. Everyone wants their little magic trick.

When I carry my guitar case without a gun inside, I still leave the gun's blanket in there, so people get used to its presence and don't ask any questions. The gun itself stays in its home behind the dryer.

My guitar case is for camping trips. We'll go on a little vacation, my case and I. This case is only for major opportunities.

I make my own straps. They're wide and short enough for me to comfortably carry a heavy weight over long distances. I do my daily push-ups with my case on my back; sometimes empty, sometimes full.

I conduct tests with different camera angles, using my cellphone for the front and a tiny second camera for the rear, snapping pictures both on foot and on my bike. I compare results with and without the case. Only after I've observed the same reaction four different times am I satisfied that the case is invisible.

It's a lot of effort just to conceal my weapon. It goes without saying that to carry a guitar around, you also have to know how to play it. I learn eleven popular songs, which I'll be able to sing around a campfire. Eight in English; three in French. There's nothing sweeter than the smell of a campfire.

The roof is asphalt with the odd patch of gravel that hasn't yet been carried away by the wind. It's covered in black tar, which explains why the building is like a slow cooker inside. I start going out on the roof often: in the morning when the sun is low, in the evening, and at night as well. Especially at night. A quotation often wrongly attributed to Margaret Thatcher says that a man who, beyond the age of twenty-six, finds himself on a bus, can count himself as a failure. I'd say the same for anyone who has never broken a rule or spent an hour of their lives observing people from above.

My building is the tallest on the block: 360 degrees of unobstructed view, the perfect perch from which to study neighbourhood life. It also affords one of the few clear views of the sky, which appears in all its immensity, even vaster than what I saw of it from the forests of my childhood. The clouds shift shapes a thousand times before receding from my field of vision, a woolly menagerie for my eyes only. I make sure that every time I go up on the roof, I have my guitar in the case with the blanket. Nothing else. The gun is for another time. Ditto the binoculars. I don't have a specific reason for visiting the roof, other than enjoying the breeze and the view, but I know it'll come. Good reasons always come to those who wait. The perfect crime is a gratuitous act. I just have to keep treading lightly.

Still, the plan could be aborted at any time. All it takes is a single person to see me, and the mission is terminated. I wouldn't be able to go up on the roof anymore, except with the purest of intentions. The plan to use the roof for an upcoming play means I have to make sure no one would ever connect me to the roof. Otherwise it's too risky. People screw up because they get lazy. They're not willing to do the groundwork necessary to get away with it. Slackers or cretins.

The bottom line is that I have to keep going up on the roof undetected, and even if someone did see me, it'd be no big deal since all I'd have to do is find a new spot. But I want to make this one work. Even if I still don't know what for... The roof is like my tree, accessible to very few people, an open-air oasis of solitude surrounded by others.

The perfect opportunity presents itself the following spring. It's an abnormally warm night and I've left my bedroom window open. The neighbours in the next building are having a party. They've been partying for the last three days. They've invited a bunch of friends over to camp out on their couch during a rock fest. I know that's what's going on because the bands playing non-stop are the festival headliners, who've been all over the radio and the TV and the papers. Since last Thursday afternoon they've been sharing their favourite albums and scintillating conversation with the whole neighbour-hood. They kick off around three in the afternoon then go out to enjoy the festival. Once they get home, the party keeps rolling until four or five in the morning. The neighbours have tried asking them to turn down the volume, with varying degrees of politeness and no success. Even when the police came, nothing changed.

Now it's early Sunday morning. Very, very early.

The music is blaring, the druggy, drunken voices loud and incoherent. A dozen people are gathered on the balcony, and at least as many in the apartment. They're barely any younger than me.

Why not?

I get dressed, grab my case, and pack my gun. Just a little air rifle, not the full-size hunting rifle. I'm just out for a little fun. I also bring the binoculars. The air is heavy; a storm is brewing. Perfect July weather, though it's only May. The buzzing of the neon lights follows me through the deserted hallways up to the door to the roof. I climb up a few steps in silence, careful not to bang my guitar case.

The roof is as black as the sky; the wet wind is warm. You can see heat lightning dancing in the distance, above the downtown skyscrapers. I stand admiring it for a couple minutes, more sensing its reverberations than actually hearing the thunder, a sort of muffled vibration that makes all the hair on my body stand on end.

I take up my position and observe my victims for half an hour. My building is nothing but a shadow: I'm certain the streetlamps can't light up my position. I pump my rifle and take aim at a hand holding a bottle of beer, leaning on the railing. The thunder rumbles, louder this time. The wind buffets up.

I press the trigger and the gun goes off, a dry clack softened by the rustling wind. The brown bottle shatters and a little blood spurts where the shards pierced the palm. Screaming and mayhem ensue. No one looks in my direction. The idea that they might have been shot at doesn't even enter their minds. The commotion raises the ire of certain neighbours, and the insults start flying in both official languages. I roll my gun up in its blanket and watch the approaching storm. Each bolt of lightning illuminates the edges of the massive cumulonimbus.

When the rain starts, I go back in. I put my clothing to soak in the washing machine and take a shower. You can't be too careful. I set the gun next to its deadlier big sister behind the dryer. By the time I'm back in bed, the night is calm once again.

Once you've shot at people and got away with it, those unambitious little plays that used to be enough start to lose their lustre. Like writing on the back of the bathroom door that the band playing at the bar is terrible, and the so-called musicians should die in their sleep and stop importuning us with their hackneyed dreams of musical glory — not so exciting anymore.

By shooting at my neighbours, I've broken one of my cardinal rules: never make a ripple in your own ecosystem. I fully understand that my plays are a little odd, but they're also harmless and easy to pull off. I get how psychologically devastating even a minor play can be. I've always avoided punishing my neighbours, close colleagues, family, or friends. Time is also key: I have to leave everyone around me enough time to forget all about me. Shooting at my neighbours was negligent and weak. I think this city's driving me crazy. Or at least pushing me to make mistakes.

Being outside and being in public aren't exactly the same thing. And yet a sizeable portion of the population doesn't understand the difference.

The pleasure of being all alone outside and possessed of the certainty that no one else will appear, and that the air and the light belong to you alone, is one many city dwellers will never know. Like people born blind, they simply don't know what they're missing. They read about and hear about other people's experiences of such solitude but are incapable of understanding what it is. And they almost never see the connection between this absence in their lives and the emptiness deep inside, which they will spend their lives struggling in vain to fill.

Enjoying the sun's rays and nature's varied sounds and tranquil beauty; walking long distances and falling asleep when you're tired without encountering another living soul: this used to be my definition of a good day. Now a good day is when the neighbours turn off their radio for a couple hours and no one is screaming. It could be a domestic disturbance, a crazy person losing their shit, a crying baby, a badly raised little girl. When you're really lucky, maybe all that at once.

I've got a long list of sounds that drive me nuts. Basically a carbon copy of the list of human suffering. These sounds make me feel like I'm being forced to sleep on a mattress stuffed with wasps whose perpetual buzzing will prevent me from sleeping until the end of time. Car horns. Sunday guitarists practising with their windows open. Dogs locked up and barking until their vocal cords tear. Parrots nervously caw-caw-cawing in their cages. All those motors that keep our world turning: cars, lawn mowers, air conditioners, circular saws, drills, sanders, mixers, juicers, coffee machines. Every time I find an empty box that once housed one of those espresso pod machines, I take down the address. I'm promising myself a major play one day, to cull each and every person who thinks it's okay to throw out their little metal and plastic pods after every cup of coffee, incapable of seeing how that massive pile of waste will impact the earth's already strained resources.

And don't get me started on other people's smells. Their garbage left out to cook in the sun. Their pea soup redolent of unwashed armpit. Their garlic and seafood recipes — just to clarify, are you literally cooking excrement? And their steaks. Their barbecues. Their cigars. That inimitable mixture of mothballs and mould wafting from old people's apartments. The stink of fried foods from restaurants. The signature soggy-bread stench of that well-known chain whose sub sandwiches are chosen on the criterion of length. Oh, I'm not done. I also hate all perfumes: those so liberally doused you can smell them fifty feet away; those that grow vinegary at the end of the day; those that have, like the people wearing them, long ago passed their best-before dates; those that would attract blood-sucking insects by the swarm in the wild but, here in civilization, merely give co-workers headaches. Verily, the catalogue of my irritants knows no end. A list with several thousand entries would include the white expectorations of hockey players next to the so-called "antibacterial" household cleaning products sprayed indiscriminately on every surface, the nail in the coffin of our already enfeebled immune systems. Let's not forget the stares of children for whom I imagine silent ends in the depths of their above-ground swimming pools. Small talk. The many daily outrages I'm subjected to, cats and their diseases, men and their obsession with pissing in alleys. Hell is other people, and all it takes is a few seconds for me to list off exactly what I hate about humanity to dispel any sense of guilt. All these people writhing like maggots: I hate them all, with a passion.

On bad days I feel like those dogs locked on roofs in the sun, despondently running around in circles, whose owners think they're treating them well while the creatures are undergoing such profound alienation that they've ceased to notice their own misery. Animals need to go down onto the sidewalk, explore a little, smell things, look around. Get out of the city, out of their homes, out of the known world. They need to be able to walk four or five hours without a thought to where they're going, slowly and without getting tired, without anyone waiting for them, without anyone chasing after them. They have to run down roads where the asphalt is chewed up and gravel turns to dirt, all the way to the end, where the trail simply ends without warning. And then keep going.

People have lost their ability to throw off the weight of the visible world. Everything we experience crushes us, stresses us, steamrolls us. But if we could just get farther away, the gravitational pull would get weaker and weaker until more massive objects pulled us toward them and pushed us elsewhere. The light of the sun, its heat, its energy — and God saw that it was good. God is everywhere and sees everything we do, with an indifference that causes us to fear him. The indifference of the universe. The indifference of everything else, its immensity, these spaces full of dark, unknown things whose effects on the course of our existence we can only guess at. God is the protective screen we are destroying in our collective murderous rage. We are indifferent to God, too, when we choose to keep our gaze downcast, because our shame prevents us from seeing the sky and the glory of creation.

Sometimes I fantasize about meeting Carl Sagan, in the same way others dream of coming face to face with Genghis Khan or John Lennon. I'd ask him what he thinks of us, of me, of my theory that all good and evil are relative, that the world has its own distinct meaning for each and every one of us, and that's what makes us unique and alone, so very alone. We're the same and different, but we are all the same in the eyes of the other so-called inferior creatures, less clever than us but with so much sharper instincts, waiting, petrified, for us to hurt them one more time.

7

Walks

Since the art of vengeance requires both energy and risk, you have to make choices. You can't punish everyone. You can't take out every offender even if, at one time or another, everyone will get on your last nerve. But there's no reason you can't have a little fun.

The worst summer of my life was my first summer in the city. It was far worse than the heat wave I'd suffer through in the brown-carpeted sweatbox apartment four years later.

At the time, I've just finished my college semester. I'm eighteen years old and still don't have a lot of translation contracts, which makes sense since I only just came up with the idea of working as a translator. Gus seems perfectly content selling his dusty books; Simone appears content spending her mom's money; and I need to find a way to be content like them since they're not about to pay my way. I find an ad. Employee wanted, customer service in a bookstore specializing in textbooks. Sounds right up my alley, on paper. But the reality won't quite align with my romantic visions of gently whiling away the afternoons in aisles stacked with the great teachings of humankind, packaged for young readers. It's not exactly a salt mine. No one's giving me forty lashes or chaining me up. But the fact remains that this summer job is pretty much the worst suffering a misanthrope such as myself could be asked to endure. My role is to supply textbooks to a spoiled and demanding clientele: rich private-school kids. Minimum wage; no tips.

We employees are posted behind a massive counter that runs along three of the store's four walls. The fourth wall houses another counter that leads to the cash register. Everyone follows the same process.

1. The client hands the employee their list of required books (textbooks and novels).
2. The employee nods their head and heads back to the warehouse, where hundreds of cardboard boxes are stacked on wooden pallets, organized by school.

3. If the box that contains a book is up too high, or is too heavy, or is for any other reason out of reach, it is deemed impossible to move by the employee, since most of us are literature students with little inclination for heavy lifting.
4. The employee reports to the client that the book they are looking for is out of stock, and will be ordered, and they'll be contacted as soon as it comes in.
5. The client collects their (small) pile of books that were within reach, complains about the service, since that's all they can do, and leaves the store.

My colleagues and I serve, on average, fifty-seven clients per day per employee. These clients fall into two categories: parents and adolescents. Note that 83 percent of these people are friendly, calm, smart, patient, and thoughtful. They instinctively understand that shooting the messenger, or issuing threats, or other such actions are unlikely to bear fruit, and may even have the opposite effect of delaying the call that will inform them that their order is ready until after the first day of school. The remaining 17 percent? I assiduously note their contact information — parents' names, children's names, address, phone number — in a little notebook I keep on my

J. D. KURTNESS

person at all times. Knowing that I possess this information gives me the strength to carry on all summer pro-
viding courteous service to happy clients. I end every
transaction with a jaunty "See you soon!"

An act of mass retribution would be a bad play. I can
already see the faces of the police inspectors, taking a long
hard look. They'd resemble the ones who questioned my
parents and me the summer of the Dupuis Creek incident.
You know: aging, balding, out of shape — typical cop.

"What do all these cases have in common? High
income, private-school kids. Aha! They all bought textbooks at the same place. Could I have a list of employees,
please? Thanks!"

But I am curious about how serious a crime needs to
be to justify a full-fledged investigation.

Buoyed by my little warm-up play with the wrapped-up
dog turd, I begin straying from the beaten path a little.
A few years have passed since my summer behind the
bookshop counter. The feeling that's stuck with me is
more curiosity than an infanticidal impulse. I make several passes in front of a massive stone mansion in a neighbourhood where annual property taxes must not be far
from the city's median income. The address matches an
entry my notebook. It's triple-underlined, along with

stars and arrows. Whoever lives here made an indelible impression.

The house sits across from a lovely park intersected by tree-lined paths. Beautiful mature trees: oaks, ash, weeping willows, silver maple, and an aspen out by a man-made pond. A few well-fed and apparently fearless ducks have moved in. Summer's almost over; the kids have gone back to school. The leaves are starting to change colour.

During the week the park is practically deserted aside from a few toddlers out with their Filipina nannies. Rarely have I enjoyed such a pleasant public observation point. I keep going to the park long after I've gathered all the information I need on our little family.

Once I know the house is empty, I familiarize myself with the exterior. Through the garden you enter a large backyard, surrounded by a fence completely covered in ivy. Three lilac trees, in dire need of pruning, bravely struggle to survive in a clump at the back of the yard. Perennials and spider plants stand tall, slowly encroaching on the space. Once nature reclaims what is rightfully hers, the entire family will be confined to the wooden deck. Under the deck there's a lawn mower, old bikes, and the lady of the house's gardening equipment. Far be it from me to perpetuate gender stereotypes, but the father, a fifty-three-year-old lawyer, doesn't strike me as the type to don flowery gloves and go digging with a pink hoe. If the state of the garden weren't a clear enough sign, the spider webs on the compost bags and terracotta pots are a giveaway that the mistress of the house gave up hoeing quite some time ago.

There's a door into the space under the deck cut directly into the wooden trellis. It closes with a hook and eye designed more to keep out skunks, cats, and racoons than to stave off thieves. Imagine my joy when I discover a basement window under the deck: a small, sliding window with no bug screen, just big enough for me to slip through. They turn the alarm system on whenever they leave the house but don't bother when someone is home. And since I highly doubt that this window is hooked up to the alarm system, and since the house is deserted at the moment, I give it a good push and bang until the spring on the plastic latch gives way. Then I put the useless latch back in place and go on my merry way.

I show up early one Saturday morning and get comfortable under the deck. I can hear the family out enjoying the sunshine. There's movement above me, comings and goings, as they get ready for their breakfast of champions. I've been under the deck three hours, but it feels like much longer. It's warm and I'm scared of falling asleep. I look at my watch, which seems to have been stuck on 9:20 a.m. for fifteen minutes. I eat my snack right underneath the family. The women and teenagers leave. I gather from their conversation that the older one needs sports gear, while the younger just needs clothes. The man stays at the house. He has to work today, but can work from home. Since he mowed the lawn last week, the chances of his doing so again today are slim. He goes back in to what must be his office, on the ground floor.

I put on my gloves and the toque that will serve as a hairnet. I used to wonder why criminals in movies always wear leather gloves. It's not a taste for luxury or style. Leather grips better than cloth. I do a little tour of the basement, quiet as a mouse. Half of it, with a bare concrete floor, is home to the hot water tank, the heating system, and some old hockey gear. I count no fewer than fourteen pairs of skates in this clutter. There's also what I imagine must be a white plastic Christmas tree, with hundreds of little red lights built right into its translucent branches. A needle-less albino tree that looks like it belongs in the depths of the ocean. I am stupefied that such a thing exists. I plug it in. It lights up like the neon sign of a bordello.

The other half of the basement displays this selfsame special blend of poor taste and opulence. Beige carpeting. An entire mirrored wall inscribed with a gilt diamond pattern. Three long, curved plaid sofas moulded to the corners of the room. A black bearskin spread out before a gas fireplace. A massive bar is the centrepiece of this scene, with eight wooden barstools lined up in front of it under orange rattan lampshades. On the golden mirrored wall behind the bar, a *katana* hangs above bottles of Scotch and crème de menthe. This elegant object, slender and light, couldn't be more out of place in this den that looks like a 1970s porn set. A stuffed swordfish would have surprised me less. Clearly I should check out people's houses more often.

Liberated from its black and red sheath, the blade cuts through the air with a satisfying whoosh. I swing it a few times in the dark room, watching my reflection in the gilded mirror on the wall. The blade shines almost blue in the weak light filtering through the rectangular windows near ceiling-height. I take a break from my part in this drama to listen for a minute. Nothing. Four minutes have elapsed since I came inside. I'm hot in my toque. The *katana* slices the sofas easily. You can barely see the long incisions in the psychedelic brown patterns on the cushions. I also make a few cuts in the carpeting near the walls and then put the katana back in its spot with a pang of regret. I didn't come here to save objects from the gaudiness of their owners' taste.

Methodically, I pour a little alcohol in the slashes in the couches, just a few shots from each bottle. I also pour a little trail of liquor between the couches, up to the window where I came in. I soak a rag in peach schnapps, tiptoe to the wall, and give the wall a pat, then toss the soaked rag out the window. I make sure everything is in place. I run up and leap out. I find the rag again, and wipe the window sill with schnapps. This isn't an episode of a procedural; I highly doubt the law enforcement professionals are going to sweep the scene in search of a fibre of clothing or, more ridiculous still, DNA. I leave the window open a crack, for my insect friends. Already, as I put a little order in my backpack, I can see the ants at work, marching in single file toward that delicious sugary scent, in the red light of the Christmas tree.

Raindrops are pinging down when I leave the patio. I take off my gloves and toque, and put on my raincoat. I casually leave the premises, with one last glance back at the luxuriant overgrown garden. I make sure no one can see me from the windows, though with my rain coat and hood up I could easily pass for a teenage boy.

The street's deserted. So is the park. I cross it one last time and walk home. I think about the *katana*. Maybe I'll come back for it one day. When I get back home, there's a message from my mother. Good news: the older Fiset brother has been released from prison.

Observing people is a vocational requirement and a personal hobby. I do it for fun because it brings me the happiness of a naturalist observing a troop of baboons. It's incredible what people will do when they think no one is paying attention. Even in public, walking down the sidewalk, people act differently when they think no one is looking. Some cling to the false belief that no one can see what they do on their balconies. I mean, if you want to fly your freak flag inside, with the curtains drawn, I get it. But outside?

I classify people into three categories. The first is by far the most sinister. I call them the drones. These people always behave in an identical manner, in the comfort of their homes or in a crowded shopping mall. They're so repressed that the idea of trying out behaviour that deviates even slightly from the norm (let alone something disgusting, or perverted, or even merely impolite) would never even enter their minds. Drones behave as if they were constantly in the limelight. Maybe they believe in an all-seeing, all-powerful god. Maybe they never stop thinking about themselves and the image they project. Maybe they just suffer from a cruel lack of imagination. Search me. People like that make my skin crawl.

Category Two takes in the vast majority of humankind. These are the normals. The ones who fart, burp, masturbate, scratch themselves, pick their scabs, pop their zits, and make faces in the mirror. They smell their fingers. They let their guts hang out. They breathe with their mouths open. They grunt. They cry. When lost in thought, some fidget like autistic children. They do these things alone and in the company of their significant others and even, for the less proud among them, in public. Extreme youth or diminished cognitive faculties (cretinism, senility, cranial trauma) also helps explain how they behave among their clans.

The third class of people are the ones who commit acts with more serious repercussions for the community. People like me. Most of the public security infrastructure and legal system is in place to reign these people in, to control and punish true deviance: child pornography, murder, financial crimes, self-harm, Munchausen's syndrome, violence directed at the elderly and other vulnerable people, exhibitionism, voyeurism, terrorism — you get the idea. For the most part, we Category Three people are sick, dangerous individuals.

Crossing paths with another member of my group is exceedingly rare. But it happens. One spring night I saw a man leaning over to pet a cat in an alley. He whispered sweetly to the animal then hugged it very hard against him, whispering shhh, shhh, shhh. I realized he was strangling it. Then he set the dead cat down on the ground, hopped on his bike, and rode off. To each their own.

I always lie low for a while before my next play. To make it easier I like to imagine that my alter ego is following me. How long, I wonder, does it take *me* to conclude that there's nothing to see when I'm observing someone? How long must I listen to the silence to be sure no one's watching?

My wariness always leads to the same fantasy. I dream of running into my double, my soulmate, the one person who understands what I'm trying to do, what's driving me, my unflagging patience and implacable logic. Someone who will love me for, and not despite, the things I do. I'm not one of those people who craves recognition. The ones who leave hints all over their crime scenes, or write open letters to the newspaper. I don't have a signature. None of my crimes resembles any of the ones that came before. I don't carve my initials in my victims; I don't piss in the corner of their rooms; and I don't leave exotic butterflies lodged in their throats or haiku folded in their superior venae cavae. The poetry of my actions is designed to resonate for me alone.

My motive is obscure. I aspire only indirectly to help bring about a certain progress for the human race. It would take a mad genius to connect the dots.

We'd trade stories and ideas, my double and I, think up a thousand large and tiny ways of exacting vengeance. Secrets grow heavy when you know you'll never be able to share them. At the same time, my extreme paranoia is what lets me sleep at night. No one knows; no one can talk. The love that surrounds me will still be there tomorrow. My parents will die of old age with tender feelings for their only daughter. My friends know they can count on me. I'll always listen to them, and they can tell me whatever they want, secure in the knowledge that I'll take it to the grave. It's no exaggeration when I say that "I'm a vault."

8

Out on Parole

I'm the observer, but I'm also under constant observation. We're all under constant observation in the panopticon of cameras, IP addresses, registries, chip cards, lists, passports, sign-ins, identifications, purchases, bonus points, and even ballots. The proof is that no matter what crap you buy at the supermarket, they'll hound you with coupons for that very same item for months. I'm very careful about my record at the public library and the video store. I may have a smart phone, but I always leave it at home, especially when I to go out for "personal reasons." There's no way I'm going to let some satellite geolocate me.

All this is just the tip of the iceberg. Brace yourself: it's about to get a whole lot worse. Anyone who refuses to play the game is going to be reduced to living isolated from the rest of the world. The time is coming when every single thing we do is going to be catalogued somewhere.

I have no illusions that I can outsmart the Machine. Instead I adopt the strategy of the microbe. Invisible to the naked eye, I scurry off at the first sight of symptoms. The Machine still can't see me, for now, no matter how penetrating its gaze. It's more like a face on a movie screen, which appears to be looking at you. The Machine is watching you with unseeing eyes. It's watching you with the keen stare of a predator sniffing the air, trying to locate a precise smell.

By spending enough time outdoors, people turn back into animals of sorts. We become one with the land when we constantly occupy it. I cease to fear danger; I become the danger. I know the road, the cadence of my walk, the texture of the ground, the exact time a given route will take, the energy each step requires of me.

At home I study maps. I always use paper maps, and I always pay cash. I use cash for everything I buy for expeditions: clothing, shoes, accessories. I only ever look at digital maps in public places on other people's computers. Ditto internet research. I want to learn as much as possible about the things I buy for specific purposes. I want the most popular models, the most common brands.

Take my Remington 870 Wingmaster. It's the "best-selling, most trusted" shotgun of all time. Commonly known as a twelve-gauge. My family's not big into guns though our neck of the woods, around Dupuis Creek, is crawling with rifles once fall comes around. Because he's not into hunting, my dad often gets taunted by the people around here. They call him an "animal lover." So when it came to firearms, I had to figure everything out for myself. Everyone on the discussion forums agrees when it comes to the 870. It sells tens of thousands of units every year in Canada alone.

I have to admit that I'm lucky: I reached the minimum age to buy a gun just a few months before the mandatory gun registry came into effect. I got my permit right before purchasing my gun. I used my student credit card, the one they give you when you're just poor enough to run up a little debt. Today I have another card, from another company, with a different number.

So I bought my gun and took the little mandatory gun-safety course. Then I let time do its work. I even bought all my ammunition well in advance. And since then I've been waiting for the perfect opportunity while the trace slowly erases itself. I practise out in the forest, far from other people.

I have an old map of the city whose folds are held together with clear tape. I use the tiny numbers on streets to estimate addresses. It's easier on my eyes. No radiation, no waves from the LCD screen; no traces. I choose not to enter the realm of the Machine whenever I can avoid it. Because every time you ask it a question and it answers, it knows. It knows and it remembers.

The trick is to avoid keywords. Don't make the same mistake as those two suburban whack jobs out to commit the perfect crime because their aunts and younger sisters weren't embracing the idea of living under sharia law in their bungalows. They were found guilty a few years ago when it was proven that they'd looked up "What's the best place to hide a body," and other key phrases, in a popular search engine.

With my method, you can be sure that the Machine loses interest after enough time has passed. It loses its scent. Time is my best friend. Time is the precious element I must respect. Since I can't control time, I have to control myself.

I always come back to the places few people venture. I can just breathe easier there. Sure, I sometimes come across other people like me, listening to the sounds of the city echoing through a silent alley. The ones who have the time to really listen, the ones you see out in the park enjoying the Tuesday afternoon sun. The ones who know how to locate the openings and cracks that let a little sky peer through, the ones who leave secret messages on concrete with stencils, chalk, or spray paint. It takes whole months for them to get comfortable with my presence. Like me, these people hate surprises.

When they see me walking by on the day of my crime, there will be no "day of the crime" in their minds. Because they won't have seen anything out of the ordinary. They'll have no idea. Everything is perfectly normal for them. SNAFU: situation normal, all fucked up. Business as usual.

Only the Machine really knows what's going on at your place, behind closed doors. You have to think about the people it represents. There are thousands of people and programs hard at work cross-referencing your data. And it doesn't take much to pique their interest. They get so bored by all these good people that they feel the need to spend their time seeking out the kind of plots where all the pieces fit together, and riling up all the people who aren't smart enough to know better. This is no time to leave a trail of bread crumbs behind. Pretty much everything you touch is now sharing your information with someone. You're just a drop in their ocean, but the Machine can turn its focus to you the moment you stray from the beaten path. The Machine is highly alert to your rhythms, your habitual way of proceeding upstream. Your light is supposed to stay the same: same colour, same wavelength, same intensity. The challenge?

Making certain neither the Machine nor anyone else can make the same connections as you. Build up your own world outside the Machine. It's still possible. It just takes ingenuity and patience.

Otherwise, you'll be caught in its net.

I read the article in my hometown paper with great interest. Mom was right: Fiset is indeed out on parole, despite being found guilty of sexual assault causing bodily harm. He was locked up for two years awaiting trial then served another three.

The newspaper gives no details of Fiset's life in prison, but I've subtitled enough episodes of *Incarcerated: North America's Worst Prisons* to know what was in store for him. Quebec had three prisons that made the list — the episode on its prisons was an edifying experience. First of all, I had to translate the prisoner's testimonials from English, and they were themselves translations of the swear-inflected French, since the English narration that had been dubbed over the prisoners' speech would now be double-dubbed over by a French-speaking narrator. It wasn't as if we could just turn up the volume of the prisoners: our viewers across the French-speaking world wouldn't understand a thing. I suspect that the more articulate criminals refused to speak on camera, leaving only their most confused brethren to tell us all about their horrible living conditions. So my job was to translate my own language. And I doff my cap to my unsung colleague who managed to accurately convey, in simple, believable English, their words. The English version was more of a help to me than the original recordings.

So the older Fiset brother spent five years in a prison at 175 percent capacity: 438 men in a building designed for 250. On weekends the gym converts to a dormitory for people serving minimum time for too many unpaid parking tickets. Rusty rebar juts out of crumbling walls. Cells designed for a single inmate now house two or three. Which means one unlucky soul has to sleep on a mattress on the ground, with his head jammed up against a seatless toilet. The blue mat looks just like the ones we used to land our somersaults on in gym class when I was a kid.

There's a special section of the prison reserved for sexual deviants. They need to be protected from the other inmates. Prison is its own world, with its own codes, governed by an ossified version of the "women and children first" ethos of panicked sailors on sinking ships. Unable to defend their own women and children, forsaken by the rest of society, men inside kill each other over rumours of pedophilia or sexual violence against women. I wonder if Fiset made some little buddies inside. If he had to lie about his crimes to come off like a hard case instead of the coward he is. The article online features his mug shot. Five years later, no one bothered to track down a more recent photo. He looks like his mom. Same face with thick features, jowls like a bulldog, lips hanging down under the weight of so much skin. The article doesn't say anything about what's happened since the release, content to rehash a brief biography and highlights from the trial.

He's our very own dangerous criminal. A local boy, born and bred on Pattenaude Farms corn and AgriNor milk. That's all anyone had to say when he was arrested. Some say he never got over his brother's death. Others insisted that he killed his own brother, his *little* brother. They just couldn't prove it.

At least the older Fiset did his dirty deeds somewhere else, off in the big city. I have no idea how he ended up here. I always had him pegged for the kind of guy who would never leave his hometown because the idea of moving away was just too much.

Back when they happened, Fiset's crimes were serious enough to warrant an article in the national newspaper. It was so typical it almost brings a tear to your eye, strictly paint-by-numbers: drugs, low self-esteem, and of course the age-old curse of the Fisets: stupidity. Fiset got completely wasted and raped a young woman who'd rejected him the previous night, after punching her a few times to soften her up. He broke her nose and ocular cavity and cracked a couple ribs for good measure.

It sure is nice to have a family that keeps you up to date on all the news from home. Because other than some top-level Hells Angels and the Rizzuto clan, the media never says much about people getting out on parole. Five years later, Fiset Sr.'s five minutes of fame consisted of a single article in the weekly paper of his little hometown, with his old photo — an article I never would have seen if my mom wasn't on top of it.

What's the right word for a man like that? A pig? That's degrading to animals. A barbarian? From the ancient Greek *barbaros,* the word means "foreigner" or, more precisely, one who speaks an incomprehensible language. Seems a little unfair to foreigners, and inaccurate to boot since I have no trouble parsing the actions of this imbecile. A monster? Is he really "a prodigy; an enormity; a marvelous manifestation of God's will"? There's nothing divine in such a disgusting act. So I'll stick to a neutral term: "target."

I wonder where he'll wash up? Think he'll maybe go *running home to mommy*?

The "internets" never cease to amaze me. My province doesn't have a public sex-offender registry, but some good Samaritans have taken it upon themselves to maintain a web page listing people you wouldn't want to run into in the park. It takes a monastic dedication to comb through all the information published on trials and sentences. All the work of upstanding citizens, the very same people who dutifully clip coupons and join search parties to reunite lost animals with their owners. I join a "Protect our Kids" group. Obviously not with my own personal profile. I use one of my four others.

These neighbourhood watchers have a head start: they've already caught sight of my Fiset in a neighbourhood southwest of my own. I was ready to phone his mother to see what he's up to; now I won't have to. I immediately start methodically surveying the neighbourhood. I suss out where he might hold his regular meetings with a parole officer. Likely a place that offers therapy for delinquents. If the rapist has to report in frequently, it stands to reason that he'll either walk or take public transit. Mapping out probable routes isn't rocket science.

My patience is rewarded ten days later. I recognize Fiset from a distance. He moves exactly as he did when he was a kid. I know he won't recognize me. Even though I find the situation amusing, I'm careful not to smile when I run into him on the sidewalk. His jeans are too big. He must have lost weight on the inside. He's still a pretty beefy guy, though, and I can imagine the rolls of fat jiggling around under his black sweatshirt. Winter's almost here, but he's not wearing a coat. I have a feeling he can't afford one. Or maybe he has other plans for what little money he has.

Fiset lives in the basement of a triplex. I'm surprised to find that the apartment is spacious. Though I haven't been inside yet, based on the size of the building I figure it must be around eight hundred square feet.

I have to act fast since guys like Fiset move around a lot, and I don't want to have to visit him four or five times. It's fall, so people are going out less often than in spring, when everyone's hungry to feel the breeze blowing away the winter months. Summer means long days and humid heat that keeps people outside in search of warm air currents. Fall is gloomier, with its dark skies and rain. It gives me more room to work.

The alley behind his apartment is home to four dogs, including two real yappers. I focus my attention on Ricky, the Boston terrier that belongs to the main-floor tenant just above Fiset's place. The dog's face reminds me of Burt Reynolds. A real pig of a hound. It makes me sick watching him guzzle down treats and then beg for more.

The simplest course of action would be to poison Ricky, and that's exactly what a less moral person than myself wouldn't hesitate to do. But that's not my style. Plus the owner's a good guy. He says hi when he sees me, whenever I go for a walk in the alley or we cross paths on the sidewalk.

He's a quiet guy in his thirties. A gamer. Lives with his girlfriend, who spends a fair part of her evenings searching for recipes on the internet for her blog, "Culinary Pleasures of the East." This online oasis of free expression is a cross between recipe ideas and a support group for obese people who refuse to be stigmatized by the dominant ideology of thin people. I signed their petition to deny airlines the right to double-charge passengers who require a second seat. It's like a handicap, so that's tantamount to discrimination.

I spend a few days working on Ricky. The little dog is nervous and territorial. Imagine his owner's surprise when, the first time we cross paths by the drugstore two streets over, his dog silently yanks the leash in my direction. I act like I don't notice, with my headphones on. I try it again, with an unzipped hoodie over a T-shirt with the *Assassin's Creed* logo, a symbol in the form of a rounded-edge triangle that we insiders recognize. Personally, I think it looks like a staple remover.

The third time we run into each other I'm carrying a thick plastic reusable grocery bag. It's full of normal everyday items; healthy, wholesome, inoffensive. The following times, I catch his eye and give him a subtle nod. Then a smile. The time after that, I venture a throaty "hi." I'm setting the scene for a few weeks from now, just in case the guy looks outside at the wrong moment. I want him to feel one thing only if he sees me walking in the alley or playing with his dog in the back-lot: a little pang of pleasure.

I stop to pet the dog, and his owner is amazed at his animal's positive reaction. Great job, Ricky. You'll be spared.

The inside of Fiset's apartment looks like a crack house. Or at least how I picture a crack house, one of those depressing places we see in the movies. The other word that comes to mind is shithole. I figure since he's been locked up for five years, the reflex of rinsing his plate has fallen by the wayside. Though it's not small, the place feels sombre and stifling. An unfinished renovation. They ran out of steam after pulling off the drywall. You can see the wiring and the plumbing running through the walls, hanging between two-by-fours. I'll have to watch my movements. The filthy carpet is intact. I couldn't tell you what colour it was if you held my hand against a burning coal.

Three rooms: bedroom, living room, and kitchen. The only door they bothered hanging inside the apartment is for the bathroom. I make sure no one is hiding in there.

Aside from the mould, not a living thing. There's no mirror. Not even a shelf. Bottles of shampoo, shower gel, and shaving cream congregate on the rim of the tub, or the acrylic floor of the shower. A brown towel is hanging on a hook. Another is lying on the ground as a bath mat.

The furniture is a mismatched collection of wood and melamine, donations and sidewalk finds. Nothing wrong with that — he's resourceful — but I doubt he's taken precautions against bedbugs. I won't sit down.

Fiset is sleeping on the couch with his jeans half unzipped. The TV's on. A stroboscope of blue light is ricocheting off his face. He's snoring despite the sound. The music isn't coming from the TV; it's playing on a brand-new stereo at the back of the room. I recognize the album. A compilation of 1990s punk hits. Some people just never move on.

The day before yesterday, I left an unmarked envelope with two hundred dollars in the rapist's mailbox. What happened? Well, there's that shiny new stereo with ridiculous plastic curves that do nothing to enhance the sound quality. Prodigy sounds way too bassy, and the voices are all rattly. The concrete floor isn't helping matters.

What he did with the rest of the cash is, as I had hoped, on display on the coffee table. Fiset's sad private party. Vodka, boxes of fruit juice, a bag of weed, a nugget of hash, rollies, a glass pipe, some brown powder, aluminum foil, a lighter, a straw, paper scraps. At least there are no needles. I hate needles.

Two Styrofoam containers, one with a splotch of processed cheese, the other with a congealed leftover poutine.

I love the word "paraphernalia": from the Latin, *paraphernalis*, meaning "crap excluded from the dowry."

In other words, the worthless crap we just can't help carrying around with us.

I figure he's been mixing his vodka with juice, adding it as he goes and drinking straight from the bottle. And while I've never touched heroin, I've seen enough people do it to know that Fiset has been chasing the dragon for two days.

I take the alley. As I cross the yard, I give Ricky a treat then go down the stairs to 1876-A. The dog follows me. I sit down with it for twenty minutes, listening to its owners talk about their vacation to the Dominican Republic. They're smoking in the kitchen and have left the window open. They're leaving Tuesday night. It's Monday. That'll make my life easier. It'll be a good time to come back. Tonight is just to make sure Fiset is still making good use of my money. If he is, I'll send him a little more next week.

The door's unlocked. I leave Ricky a bone the size of a femur, which he chews on with determination. I'm just here to take a look. Just a quick checkup and I'll be on my way.

But Fiset is snoring. I've been here fifteen minutes and he's still snoring. I can hear the wet crackling sound of Ricky's teeth on his treat. I decide it's time to make my play. I put on gloves. Lock the door. Approach the sleeping man.

I snap my fingers next to his ear. Nothing. Clap my hands. Give the couch a few kicks. The rapist doesn't stir. Opportunity is knocking, hard. I close the blinds, hold-overs from before the renovation. I place the blankets on the nails that are waiting for them so no one can see through the windows. It's after nine at night anyway, so everyone else's windows will be covered with curtains or blinds. I could carry out my plan in broad daylight and no one would notice. But I can't get impatient, I have to stay careful.

I move all the furniture away from the couch so I won't bump into anything. I can't believe my luck, though situations like this are exactly the reason I never leave my house without hockey tape, an X-acto knife, gloves, and a toque. I don't wear a balaclava, too clichéd. Plus my face gives me a little extra time. People panic when they see a balaclava, and adrenalin is my worst enemy. My sweet little face, on the other hand, leaves me a window to take action. The lights are turned off before anyone has time to see what I look like anyway.

Not wearing a balaclava is also one less thing for me to think about. Imagine how embarrassed I'd be if I fled the scene and forgot my face was covered by a balaclava. A toque, on the other hand, can always pass as an eccentricity.

I bind his hands with tape. He doesn't wake up. Then his feet. The TV's gleam is the only light on us. I delicately drape one of his T-shirts over his eyes, folded in half. A black Slipknot T-shirt. I realize I'm humming the melody of the song playing in the background.

I wrap the T-shirt around the armrest, to immobilize his head. I pinch his nose a few seconds until he stirs a little and then starts snoring again. I use almost an entire roll of hockey tape to tie him to the couch. The smell of bilious vodka on his breath gives me the feeling that he isn't going to put up much of a fight.

A song I really like comes on. The TV's showing a rerun of an afternoon show, with guests gushing over a sardine and clementine salad. I hear the upstairs tenants walking from their kitchen to their bedroom, then the bathroom. A shower or a bath. The pipes fastened to the ceiling register a collective protest.

Finally, I take what's left of my hockey tape to cover Fiset's mouth. I hold his jaw with my forearm, and the back of his head is stuck against my abdomen. I plug his nose with the other hand and wait. He fights a little but not much. I hope he won't throw up; I'm not in the mood to wash my clothes in his revolting shower.

I wait seven long minutes before letting go. His chest doesn't fill up. It smells bad, really bad. Like shit. I let Fiset go, a perilous enterprise since he has shat himself. *Gotta keep them separated.* There's no vomit in his mouth, though. He only leaked out one end. I turn him over on his side, toward the back of the couch. His pants are half off, his back full of liquidy excrement. I'm the only person in the world who knows that both the Fiset brothers died with their asses up in the air.

I put the furniture back where it was, and rub away the marks its legs left on the carpet. I roll all the tape up into a ball, put it in a plastic bag, and hide it at the bottom of my bag. I take the weed. I take the empty envelope I sent Fiset, deformed from being pawed by his big moist mitts. I also notice a slender lined notebook with maple leaves on the cover, the kind used by schoolchildren. It's

full of Fiset's scribbles. Maybe an exercise for his therapy.
I put it in my bag too.

I turn down the music. Change the TV channel to
one with round-the-clock programming. I resist the
temptation to put on the Reality Channel. It's a rerun
tonight: the (true) story of a woman whose face was torn
off by her neighbour's monkey. Poor woman.

9

Humidex

I walk fifty-six minutes before throwing the ball of used tape in a municipal garbage can. It's 10:44 p.m. when I get back home. I put my clothes in the washing machine: just a soak for now. I don't want to wake up the neighbours with the machine. I take a nice long shower. I go to sleep.

Tomorrow is the first day of vacation. Three weeks of absolute freedom. No dialogue to translate; no deadlines; no meetings. I'll have to find a new project since the Fiset play wrapped up ahead of schedule. Priorities. I eat breakfast. Give my parents a call: it's important to keep up the family ties. Do my laundry. Empty out my backpack, hang it on the clothesline to air it out. Though I can't quite chase the smell of a dead body evacuating itself, it's only in my mind, and the simple act of washing my clothes makes me feel better. My work done, I try to enjoy my booty.

A little under a gram of crushed-up bud, enough for a pretty fat joint. I hope it's good, not that crap cut with parsley or whatever the kids sell downtown. It smells all right, if pretty mild. A far cry from Gus's industrial-strength shit.

Lying on my stomach on my bed, I flip through the blue notebook. I have to laugh. I've dug up the CD that was playing yesterday. I knew I had it somewhere. The weed is good. The notebook, not so much. It's full of designs for tattoos and songs I suspect of being the rapist's original compositions. Disappointing. No revelations, just the run-of-the-mill platitudes of a lowdown bastard. The guy was a waste of air. He didn't deserve the oxygen produced by a single dandelion.

I take the battery out of the smoke detector. Open the kitchen window. Burn the notebook slowly in the sink.

I decide it's time to go for a walk, enjoy my new-found freedom, and figure out what to do next. I try out a new suburb named after one of the Apostles, farther to the south and to the west. It's hemmed in by three railroad tracks and two highways. I haven't spent much time there up to now since getting there on foot is an ordeal. You have to take a tunnel after walking along the side of busy road that passes over the viaduct supporting the railroad. The noise is deafening and the place smells like pigeon shit. Forty metres in a dark, humid tunnel along a path strewn with garbage floating in little puddles of water that never fully evaporate. The place is also full of little strawberry-sized snails. I smell them more than I hear them as I crush their shells under my boots. Sorry, but there's just too many to walk around

I emerge from the tunnel and keep walking. I can still hear a regular vibration that must terrorize the poor earthworms. Two thin, dirty little boys are playing in a back alley. The older of the two is banging on the asphalt with a hammer. They're brothers. They have the same sneakers and the same faces. It's the older one busting up the pavement while the younger one watches him with that particular adulation of young boys watching their older brothers.

Slow, muffled blows, *tock, tock, tock*, stripping away the asphalt around a ragweed plant.

"Guys! You have to pull out the plant by the roots." I'm trying to be helpful.

"But look, it's about to flower! Look at the buds."

The younger one this time, proudly pointing his filthy hands toward the top of the stem. The other one just keeps banging away relentlessly: *tock, tock, tock, tock.* He's slowly enlarging the space in which the weed proliferates, brow furrowed with effort. He doesn't care about allergies. I let them do what they want. I don't have allergies. And I'm not about to make them kill this plant whose growth they must have been following for weeks. The sun is high in the sky. I leave them to their gardening.

I haven't taken more than five steps when I hear a woman yelling to bring the hammer back before their father shows them what happens when you take his stuff without permission. She bursts into the alley. Her skin is unnaturally tanned. She has that dry, brittle look of people who drink instead of eat. Stick arms, visible tendons in her neck, even though she's young. She's wearing a white T-shirt that says "Everlast" at tit level. If I weren't so surprised, I'd laugh out loud.

"Damn it, what are you two up to now?"

She gives the older one a hard swat on the arm, and he coughs up the hammer without a peep. The younger brother instinctively retreats toward me. That's when his mom sees me. She stares a second then goes on her way. Yanks out the allergenic plant and goes back into her yard, dragging her kids by the shoulders. The hammer stays on the ground. I move along.

I walk by a bar whose aroma of urinal cake smell wafts all the way out to the sidewalk. A limping grey cat scurries off to cower under a porch. It licks itself in vain. Its wound is bleeding, and it's suffering. When the cat lifts its leg, anyone can see that there's nothing natural about the angle. Down the street, three kids are pretending to shoot each other with empty water pistols.

I quickly make my way through the neighbourhood, which isn't proving welcoming. One last graffito bids me goodbye: "My brother's dead. I didn't even like him."

I discover a secret shortcut. Someone has cut out a section of the chain-link separating the tracks from the rest of the world. I count five crows querulously pecking. Despite the sun and the fresh air, there's something sinister about this place. I don't stick around. What interests me is what I'll find on the other side of the tracks. This enclave is just an escape route for once my work is done.

Opulent homes, immaculate lawns. Another language, at least on the street signs. It's 3:00 p.m. when I find myself in front of the home of Richard Bonenfant, president and CEO of ShaleCorp Energy Inc. — that's if the corporate information on the business register is up to date. The other board members' personal addresses are also written in the register, available to the public, free of charge, at any time. This time I'll get to see the havoc wreaked by my work. In any case, extra security measures are always temporary.

I'll be back, Dick.

Energy. En-er-gy! Whatever would we do without it? Why, we'd perish in the most abject suffering, that's what. The world would be plunged into chaos. We'd devour ourselves like swine deprived of their dose of antibiotics. People are so afraid, so cold. They'd rather suffocate than change. And can we really blame them?

I could have chosen animal rights as my cause, but then cruelty has always been an integral part of human nature. There are just too many people to choose from. And then where to draw the line? Would I kill everyone who eats at McDonald's? What about KFC? Ranchers? Slaughterhouse employees? The executives of the agrifood conglomerates? Their majority shareholders? The syndicates who invest in the multinationals? The politicians and governments who don't take action? The people who vote them in?

There's no such thing as absolute integrity. Even vegans are ill-positioned to cast the first stone. Tea and coffee, no matter how fairly traded or organic it claims to be, comes to us from faraway places with a massive carbon footprint. Growing soy and almonds sucks up all the groundwater. Demand for ancient grains and exotic legumes destabilizes markets and steals the livelihoods of African subsistence farmers. And let's be honest: no one likes a do-gooder!

Don't get me started on the entertainment industry. Tigers whipped until they perform on command, dancing monkeys in porcelain masks, horses spurred on until they dislocate their legs, starved whales, and asthmatic epileptic dogs with lumbar strain, bladder cancer, and conjunctivitis. Doves asphyxiated in the bottoms of black top hats. Bullfighting. Frozen fish forgotten at the bottoms of ponds. Puppy mills. Caged birds.

To blow up an aquarium and all its occupants would take a bomb. Too much hassle. Truth be told, I'm a little bit lazy. ShaleCorp is an obvious symbol whose CEO just happens to live a few kilometres from my home.

Alone.

If something smells fishy about all this (who knows, I may have omitted a detail or two, or skipped a clue), you have Serge Alwyn to blame. He's my fall guy. Why Serge? A few years ago I heard him on a radio call-in show, making some comment about Formula One racing. His take was that people in the future would look back on Formula One the way we look back on dogfights today: a boorish, backwards practice. A man after my own heart; an argument not unlike my own. The difference between him and me is that I've never shared my deepest convictions on prime-time public radio. It goes without saying that bringing him in is strictly a last resort. The need to point my finger at an innocent person guilty only of sharing a few of my ideas in no way fills me with joy.

I pack a snack: nuts, water, yoghurt in a reusable container, and dried fruit. As always, I scrupulously avoid things that need to be peeled, things that drip, things that smell, and anything that makes noise when you unwrap it. I also brought along a special little drink for Mr. Bonenfant. It's an unusually mild October day: warm, but not too hot. Perfect. I don't want him to lock himself inside with the air conditioning on. I need a nice day, the kind where you want to be outside on a Friday night.

I wait for my friend in his yard, shielded by the shed and the hum of his pool filter. It reminds me of the halcyon days of my youth, with fewer trees and more flowers. Bonenfant must pay a gardener to take care of all this rockery. The garden is chock full of plants: forget-me-nots, hostas, coneflowers, tiger lilies, day lilies, lemon lilies, clematis, ferns, rhododendrons, and a wealth of other species I don't know are all vying for space. It was worth the walk. I hope I don't get soaked by the automated sprinkler system.

I'm eating what's left of my cashews when he comes through the patio door. He puts his cellphone down on the table, a massive brushed-glass affair. He sits down with a bottle of mineral water and starts reading *Forbes*. What a walking cliché! At least he isn't watching Belarusian porn on his laptop, like last week (though to be fair the country of origin is a guess). At forty-nine, the man looks thirty-five. He's barely even greying at the temples. Tall and thin. A treadmill junkie. Every night he runs on the spot while watching the 11:00 news on American cable TV. His forgettable looks are enhanced by expensive suits and fashionable haircuts. This evening all he's done is take off his jacket and roll up his shirt sleeves to his elbows.

His backyard is so big you'd need to park a crane next door to peer in and see what he's up to. I note the angle he sits down at. A few minutes go by. He gets up to go inside for a bit. At least, that's what I figure since he's left his stuff outside. Showtime.

On my last little visit I pulled a brick out of the wall of the flower bed that runs along the shed. I left it there, waiting for me when I'd need it. I take a position behind the wall, to the right of the glass door. He comes out and sits down again. I clock him on the back of the head, with a satisfying thud. He collapses immediately, upper body thrust forward. There's a little blood. The sun has almost gone down.

The idea isn't to kill him. I just need him to remain unconscious for a few minutes. If I hit him a little too hard, it's no big deal, but I am proud of myself when I hear him still breathing. I take his phone. No password. He must be too busy for that. I turn it off and put it in my pocket. I drag him inside, no small feat. My hours spent at the gym are rewarded, though, and I manage to pull him several metres in under two minutes and get him over the patio door ledge.

I tie him up with some strong rope. I know how to make knots, all kinds of knots. There are YouTube videos. I tie knots quickly. I practise regularly.

I bind his mouth with duct tape. That's enough for now. He can wake up when he wants; it'll be no skin off my back. I stand in the living room and set a password for his phone. I like the idea that he won't be able to use it in the highly unlikely event that he regains consciousness and tries to call for help. I check out his agenda. Nothing planned for this weekend. I check his text messages and emails. I want to know whether I'm going to be interrupted. Nothing so far. I keep the device close at hand, in case that changes.

Under the kitchen sink, I find a cloth that I moisten to wipe up any traces of blood. The prisoner's wound has stopped bleeding, but it's left a mark on the patio table, the pressure-treated wood of the deck, and the living room floor. I take my time scrubbing out the grooves in the PVC for the bug screen and glass door. The chlorinated water from the pool works wonders. I give the brick a good soak before putting it back with the others.

The sky is pink and gold. I can hear the blackbirds singing and a lawn mower groaning in the distance. The neighbours are having pre-dinner drinks in their yard. I can hear them laughing. I pick up everything left on the table. I go out looking for my bag behind the shed. I wring the rag out over the place where I was waiting, to simulate rainfall and cover my tracks.

The magazine goes in the recycling bin; the mineral water in the fridge. I draw the curtains. Lock the doors and windows. Turn on a few lights. I'm doing the tour of this mansion when the phone vibrates in my pocket. A certain "Anita" just sent a text: their date was pushed back from 8:00 to 9:00. She wanted to give him a heads-up so he wouldn't get there too early. I say I can't make it, blame it on a headache and a tough week, which isn't too far from the truth. She answers with a platitude and a smiley face.

I drag him to the basement. Going down stairs with a 175-pound unconscious man is a real workout. I'm almost tempted to pour ice water over his head to wake him up so he can give me a bit of a hand. Crime requires much more exercise than people think. Finally, after thirty minutes of intense effort, I manage to get him down the stairs.

The basement has a giant home theatre, a bathroom, and another unfinished section where the hot water heater and heat pump are housed. A few framed-in but unfinished walls sit waiting for their viscera to be covered with drywall.... All the house's systems seem to converge here. I feel around in search of the fixture most solidly attached to the walls and settle on a metal pipe that doesn't yield to any of my attempts to move it. I use it to immobilize Bonenfant's legs with rope. I leave him just enough slack to grab a water bottle, or to reach his cellphone if he's willing to dislocate a limb for the cause.

I sit him down against the wall studs and fasten his neck to a cross-brace with a U-lock. Who said TV was a waste of time? Even if he manages to wriggle free, his neck isn't going anywhere. He'd have to saw through the board, or the lock, or his neck.

I go upstairs. The fridge and pantry are a cornucopia of salty snacks: shaved ham, Genoa salami, Triscuits, chips, and a delicious-looking hunk of blue cheese. I place the feast on the ground next to my victim, along with a big plastic bottle labelled "Spring Water" that contains tap water mixed with gasoline. Another little trick I picked up on TV. I look around a bit and find a sleeping bag. Its job will be to absorb sounds, like yelling. I complete the soundproofing by stuffing all the basement windows with cushions. I grab some household cleaner and get to work, just in case. Sure, I'm wearing gloves, but why not clean anyway? I've got nothing but time. I readjust my toque. I wash the floor, the plastic bottle, the salty snacks, the place where I set my backpack down. Ditto the rope and duct tape over the prisoner's mouth, which is gradually getting covered in slobber. Our president and CEO is still sawing logs. I put away the cleaner. Rinse and wring out the rag. Dump it in the laundry hamper.

I cover my victim in a thick wool blanket I found in one of the bedrooms. I close the door leading to Bonenfant's hideout, which isn't easy since the sleeping bag gets caught in the door frame. I make sure the air conditioning is off. I turn on the home theatre system and choose a twenty-four-hour news channel. I turn up the volume. I go back to the ground floor. The lights are on a timer, to deter burglars.

He has $380 in his wallet. I only keep the twenties, for a total of $180. I leave the red and brown bills, which attract far too much attention to use to buy an ice cream cone. Muffled sounds from the basement. Something's squirming down there. Reassured, I leave the house, handling the patio door with care. It's night now. I let a little air in for a few minutes, to spread the molecules around a bit after spending four hours in this big empty house. The only sound I can hear now is the lapping of the pool. It's a beautiful clear night. A slender crescent moon glides over the rooftops.

I methodically inventory my bag, by feel, the way I've practised. Once my eyes adjust to the darkness, I'll take off my toque while ensuring that that not a single hair falls off. The fence closes behind me with a metallic click. I take off my gloves. Wait five minutes. Nothing moves. I walk toward the tracks. In the middle of the enclaved neighbourhood, I see two raccoons feasting on the contents of two gutted orange garbage bags. I throw my toque and gloves in the garbage juice, and stomp all over them so they're thoroughly saturated. I bid the night creatures good night, and leave them what's left of my snack.

I hit the road again. Minus the bottle, the lock, the clothing, and the food, I feel light as a feather. The keys to the lock get tossed down a storm drain six blocks from my apartment. The clinking they make when they hit the ground is the sweet sound of success. Tomorrow I'm meeting friends for breakfast. It's supposed to be unseasonably hot and humid this weekend. Health authorities recommend drinking lots of water.

10

Indian Summer

Not everyone realizes that killers with any ambition need to be in tip-top mental and physical condition. It's just as important as planning. You have to be able to walk quickly for extended periods of time. Deal with stress without panicking, getting tired, or succumbing to exhaustion. Endure heat and cold, humidity, wet feet, the sweat that plasters our T-shirts to our torsos and our jeans to our thighs. Know your limits. Control your breathing so no one hears you. It's critical that no one can take us down in the darkness. We can't afford to be picky. We have to put up with mosquitoes and other biting insects. Wear sturdy shoes: popular models we buy on sale and then, like everything else we own, let sit a while before using them again. That way they'll never find us. I, for one, am still at large. I'm in my living room eating Cheerios and watching the news. They found the body Thursday. There's talk of a homicide. The police are tight-lipped. Because they've got nothing.

I'm a huge fan of the great outdoors. Friends and family would describe me as an avid hiker and camper. They think it's my northern roots. They think I'm going to be a back-to-the-lander when I can no longer take the idea of translating another season of *Dwarves: Larger Than Life*. I'm an organized, trustworthy young woman. On time. Helpful. People even enjoy my slightly twisted sense of humour. I never let a good joke go to waste. Like when I helped some friends set up their modem: since they complained about being subject to the sound of their neighbours' conjugal bouts, I named their network 4553StJude_wehearyoufucking. Three years later, that one still gets trotted out at every dinner party.

Seduction is also a big part of the job. I never seduce my own victims. I hate them too much for all that jazz. By the time I touch them, it's already game over. But I do seduce other people in a variety of ways. Love makes you blind; love makes you stupid. Love lets you accept lies by denying untruths. Being suspicious is the root of suffering, and very few people actually want to suffer. When in doubt, I imagine that a little bit of mental gymnastics will keep everything afloat. No one wants to be betrayed. We look down on people who get duped. Like a magician, I focus people's attention away from where the sleight of hand occurs.

Lying comes as naturally to me as breathing. Second nature. I've been building parallel worlds so long that my balancing act requires as little effort as digesting my lunch: it's a reflex. It happens all on its own, without my having to think about it. The main factor motivating me to avoid getting caught, aside from preserving my liberty, is my parents. I just couldn't put them through that. They wouldn't understand. Or, worse still, they might.

My lovers have never suspected a thing. *Wow, you're really into it tonight. Yeah, must be the heat. You smell good, like summer. Take off your shorts, honey. Leave the curtains open. I want to see you. No one ever looks in that window.* Just as you never look behind the dryer. That's where I hide my gun, in a leftover length of aluminum exhaust piping that sort of looks like a flexible caterpillar full of spider webs. Perhaps one day a perspicacious scientist will find, at one of my crime scenes, eggs belonging to a rare species of spider whose last remaining habitat is my apartment. He'd then follow the trace all the way back to me. But real life isn't an episode of *CSI*. Good thing, too! *What are you thinking about? Nothing, kiss me.*

I understand how athletes display heightened sexual appetite after a victory, at least the ones whose genitals haven't been shrivelled to nothing by steroids. Despite my aching muscles and exhaustion, I'm always euphoric after I make a play.

Public life, private life, secret life.

Let's take a quick break to lay two misconceptions to rest.

One: silencers. The movies have everyone thinking you can just pop one on the end of your gun and a bullet shot at one thousand metres per second will sound like a kitten landing on a pillow. Wrong. Best case, a silencer can diffuse the blast and create confusion as to the shooter's point of origin.

Two: cigarettes. Due to their the photogenic nature, you always see your protagonist lurking in the shadows and lighting up a smoke while his victim serves himself a Scotch and undoes his bow tie, oblivious to the tragic end lying in store. Sorry, no. Unless your sense of smell has been dulled by forty years of two packs a day, or you had a terrible accident that bashed your face all the way in to your sinuses, the smell of a cigarette is like lighting a flare in a storm.

Needless to say, neither silencers nor cigarettes are part of my arsenal.

Since I'm no longer content to disguise my murders as accidents, suicides, or overdoses, additional precautions are required. I'm planning a big outdoor play. And being outside means you can't fully control your environment. I have to anticipate every last possibility and plan out a series of different actions for each potential scenario.

I take steps so investigating officers will think I'm a man. Buy generic clothing in warm, durable fabrics, at a store catering to construction workers. A pair of work-boots that are too big for me. I try them on to see how comfortable they are. Claim I'm buying them for my brother, a gift to celebrate getting his journeyman's ticket. I make minor adjustments to the soles, enough to disguise my footprints and temporarily confound the crime scene investigators.

I take long bike rides. Reconnoitre the site on my second visit. Skid marks delineate the borders of the area. My information was good. The idea came to me as I flipped through one of the daily papers and came upon a highly instructive article entitled "Driving 300 km/h and Living to Tell the Tale." A group of guys who are cognitively impaired and don't realize it post photos and videos of their exploits on social media. A few hours elapse between the posts and the people involved figuring out that they could make a secret group. Plenty of time for me to get a good start on my mental notes.

It's seventy-eight kilometres from my apartment to the "secret" drag strip of dusty road. Four and a half hours of leisurely biking. It's important to conserve energy, so I don't arrive exhausted. Eight kilometres away there's a campground that also has a few hotel rooms. I make a reservation in person, under a fake name, for a single night's stay two weeks from now. I leave a cash deposit. I keep my receipt. The road runs east to west, connecting one small village to another, but since the highway performs the same function, no one really uses it. Especially not at night. Hence its popularity with amateur drag racers.

To the north you have to cross eighty-three kilometres of mixed forest before the next settlement, a hamlet of 133 souls eking out a living from ecotourism and government subsidies. Virgin forest, basically, save a handful of hunting cabins, with eighteen lakes and hundreds of creeks. A paradise for hunters and anglers, though hunting is forbidden on the date I'm planning, since it's mid-October and the "killing" season ends in three days. Of course, the big game I'm after isn't covered by any of the permits issued by the province's ministry of forests, wildlife, and parks.

To the south are swampy wetlands full of tree frogs and pussy willows, all the way up to the highway. Probably the future site of a shopping centre, where you'll be able to buy an eight-dollar shirt sewn by tiny brown hands. For now, the swamp is the object of a dispute between two municipalities. The legal battle has been raging for four years and involves three levels of government, two citizen's coalitions, a regional chamber of commerce, and three environmental groups. Yet I've never come across a single soul out here.

The plain isn't completely flooded. It's still possible to walk around and keep your feet dry if you know the terrain. I know the terrain. I spend hours and hours there, by day and at night, under rain and sun, buffeted by winds. I count the number of footsteps it takes, both ways. Soon I can do the walk blindfolded, without getting stuck in any kind of weather. I'll be long gone by the time they clear a path in the tall grass and realize they have to call in the dog squad and helicopters or spend weeks mucking around in a swamp.

Aside from a few outliers, most people are completely unexceptional. There aren't many great scientists, journalists, artists, or leaders. Picture the public figures you know. Then imagine the other 7.3 billion people in the world you've never heard of. Finally, add the pile of one hundred billion dead bodies our species has produced since we figured out what little we know. It's stiff competition. *Mes semblables, mes soeurs*: we all hold down jobs that we hate to some extent. One popular adaptation strategy to temper the burning desire to gouge your eyes out is soldiering on "for the family." Good parents are prized under the dominant ideology. You can tell you're good parents if your offspring survives. It appears that being extremely busy and tired also boosts your child-rearing aptitude coefficient. Keeping kids alive is a full-time job. Imagine the catastrophe when parents realize they've produced an imbecile. The law allows you to put your dog down if it exhibits dangerous behaviour, or even if you just aren't feeling it anymore, but you can't gas the fruit of your loins when they start displaying clear signs of idiocy.

The fundamental questions are these: Is a cretin a cretin by choice? Are assholes responsible for their assholery? If some waste of flesh pulverizes his frontal lobe behind the wheel of a Honda Civic with purple underlighting, should we collectively pay to feed him through a tube for the rest of his days?

I'll never run short of projects. I can't get enough of the comment threads on news sites. How stupid do you have to be to use your own name?

Work boots. Unremarkable shoes. Warm clothing (two outfits). Toque. Gloves. Water. Food. Wallet. Binoculars.

Compass. Hunting knife (a compromise, just in case). Rope. Hunting rifle. Ammunition (two boxes, forty rounds). Case. Guitar. Blanket. Watch. Mini first aid kit (you never know). Maps. Lighter. Bike. Smile.

There's morning frost on the ground, shining like crystal under the first rays of the sun. This show won't last. The frozen dew will evaporate soon. Already I can't see the steam on my breath. I've taken off my hoodie. I set off before dawn, my favourite time to travel. It's Saturday. Since I left town, I've seen only two cars. They were full of young people on their way home to bed.

Thanks to the unseasonably warm weather, leaves still cling to their branches. A gorgeous landscape, bathed in lambent autumn light; a forest daubed in yellow, orange, and red. Farmers' fields stretch on either side of the secondary road I've chosen. The harvest is over, and in a few weeks the snow will come. Cold already grips the brown earth. The crunching of my bike tires on the gravel is the only sound I hear. The birds that live in these parts have already left for the winter.

No, not quite: when I get to the top of a little hill, I see thousands of white points in the middle of a field. White geese slowly waking up, warmed by the sun's rays. They'll breakfast on the crumbs of the harvest then take off in a deafening beating of wings. I stop to watch them. Nature has a way of setting the perfect scene.

I hide my bike behind a wild rose bush in full bloom, fifty metres from a little dirt path between two fields. It's not even 8:00 a.m. and the sun's already pounding down. I walk with my guitar case and my backpack until I reach the spot where the road ends and the marshland begins.

I count my steps and retrace the labyrinthine path to an observation point on the side of the road that the drag racers use. I open the case and pull out the gun, which is wrapped in a big plastic bag. I stash the weapon and the ammunition. My load lightened, I travel back along the same path and pick up my bike. I have all day to visit the area and make friends.

The sun slowly clouds over. The yellow light turns milky. Some people say the phenomenon is caused by forest fires a few hundred kilometres to the north. There's even a trace of burnt wood in the air. It hasn't rained in weeks, and the land has become a tinderbox.

At the campsite I strum a few chords. In under twenty minutes my first admirer shows up: He tells me his friend is turning eighteen, and a bunch of his buddies are up here to celebrate. With my baby face, I have no problem shaving a few years off my actual age. They invite me over to their campfire, which they're keeping a close eye on in these dry conditions.

The forecast calls for storms tonight. I offer my hotel room if it gets so bad their tents can't handle the rain. I say I'm out here after a recent breakup, needed a change of scene, a little fun. They tell me all about their lives. I discreetly make myself responsive to their clumsy seduction efforts. I drink very little though no one notices. After midnight several of them pass out. I pick up the most persistent and take him back to my room. He's cute, and he's drunk, and he passes out on the bed, fast asleep without my even having to make him any promises. If he wakes up, I'll pretend I went back to the fire. I'll seduce them all one at a time, if that's what it takes.

The road is deserted, the night black. I ride my bike, scarcely able to see where I'm going. I can just barely make out the line marking the centre of the lane. I follow it.

I hear them before I see them. First their music, then their voices. They're talking loud and laughing. Revving their engines. There's no shortage of noise to drown out the sounds I'm making. I count nine people total: four men, five women. Each has a cellphone. I'll have to destroy those; who knows what they could catch on film or snap a photo of. Two sports cars with oversized wheels sit at the starting line. I'll wait for them at the finish line. In the moonless night, I'm invisible.

Two new cars show up and six more people spill out. I should have brought more ammo. I'm not a good enough shot to hit a target moving three hundred kilometres per hour. So I wait. The winner will be first served.

Someone gives the signal. I close my eyes to avoid being blinded by the headlights. They pass me and slow to a stop. I open my eyes and take aim. Four bullets for two men. A sound like firecrackers. I reload and jump down to the bottom of the rock. Two girls, undoubtedly the drivers' girlfriends, are screaming and crying. One is trying to call for help, but the blood makes her fingers slip. I take aim again. Four rounds for her.

They've turned down the music at the other side of the drag strip. People are running around, screaming. Phones are ringing but no one answers. I'll come back for those later. I reload again and run toward the light and noise along the routes I've memorized, a few metres off the path. Six people are walking toward the racers. Four bullets in the magazine. I let them pass, then come back behind them. I plant my feet firmly on the pavement to get a better shot. I press the trigger, four times.

Two men are down and no longer moving, another is jumping around, and a woman is staring confusedly at the blood on her hand. A man and a woman watch me as I reload, then something clicks and they start running. Wrong way: they're headed for the swamp. They're no more than twenty metres in and already in up to their thighs. I pick them off like clay pigeons.

I load two more bullets and listen. The two survivors are moaning and crying out to their friends for help. I leave them there. I'll finish them off in a few minutes.

I set off in pursuit of the other five. They're on the way, sitting in two cars driving slowly toward the midpoint in the strip. I use the same technique: let them pass, then come up behind them. They jump out of the vehicles and rush over to the bodies splayed out in the middle of the road. The cellular network must be weak; none of them have managed to call the authorities.

Everyone is looking frantically all around, blinded by the headlamps. I shoot three of the men, and let the two survivors flee northward. They're fast but loud. I finish off the wounded with my knife. Slit their throats, and their silence helps direct me to the fugitives. I leave my gun by the road and start running along, guided by the sound of their bushwhacking.

My oversized boots slow me down, but it still takes less than two minutes to get to the point where I can hear my prey breathing. One is faster than the other, but her sense of compassion gets the better of her survival instinct. She offers her friend a hand, to help her keep up the pace. She trips and falls. The other one tries to drag her to her feet; I pounce. It's not a fair fight: tempered steel against soft, warm human tissue.

They outnumber me, and they have adrenalin on their side, but everything else is in my favour. I stab with all my strength, until I feel the resistance of bone. They squeal like animals. I don't stop until nothing is moving any more. It's started to rain. The water's moisture cools the blood. My shoulder aches from the recoil. I also got punched in the head in the struggle. I think my lip is bleeding. I put away my knife and search my victims for phones. I only find one. I stomp on it till the light goes off.

Fifteen bodies, thirteen phones. It seems like I've been here for hours; in fact only twenty-eight minutes elapsed between the moment I started shooting and when I came back to pick up my things. Once I'm sure I have everything, I set off northward. I walk toward the campsite. Do a few detours so as not to leave a rectilinear path. It's pouring rain. The sound is soothing.

The heavy rain tapers off to a soft pitter-patter moistening the forest floor. The lake catches me by surprise; I even wade in a few steps before I realize. It's a small body of water banked by a thin strip of pebble beach. A glassy, silent mirror overhung by tall fir trees. The sky clears while I remove my clothes, giving way to the white light of the several thousand stars visible to the naked eye. When I take my boots off, I feel a heaviness in my right ankle. I pull off my sock and find a swollen leach feeding on me, its suckers latched onto my Achilles heel. Eventually it falls off, and I stomp on it. It's been on me a while. I must have picked it up in the swamp. I soak my dirty clothing. My load of laundry floats to shore, a lumpy black mass slowly sinking. I listen to the thousands of silences presaging the coming of dawn. There's no wind, no animal cries.

I swim to the middle of the lake. Floating on my back, I stare up at the milky smear that is our galaxy. The stars are twinkling arrhythmically. The fireflies are taking it easy until spring comes. An inaudible signal, a subtle hint of the coming of dawn, and the forest launches into its matinal concert. The collective song of hundreds of birds rises toward the heavens, a celebration whose secret is known only to nature. I watch a firefly recede into the distance, until I can no longer say whether it's just too far away for me to see, or whether its light has stopped shining.